Princess's Forbidden Holiday Fling

Jennifer Faye

Recycling programs
for this product may
not exist in your area.

ISBN-13: 978-1-335-59648-2

Princess's Forbidden Holiday Fling

For questions and comments about the quality of this book, please contact us at CustomerService@Harlequin.com.

Harlequin Enterprises ULC
22 Adelaide St. West, 41st Floor
Toronto, Ontario M5H 4E3, Canada
www.Harlequin.com

Printed in U.S.A.

Princesses of Rydiania

Out of the palace into the limelight!
Three royal sisters, one fairy-tale dream!

When Prince Istvan fell in love and stepped out of the line of succession, the lives of his three sisters changed irrevocably.

Princess Gisella became Crown Princess, and her younger sisters, Beatrix and Cecelia, were expected to step even further into the royal spotlight and carry the monarchy into the future.

But as they await their brother's royal wedding and Gisella's coronation, the princesses all begin to question their place in the palace, and discover that their true heart's desire might not be exactly as they imagined...

Read Cecelia and Antoine's story in
His Accidentally Pregnant Princess

Discover Beatrix and Rez's story in
Royal Mom for the Duke's Daughter

And check out Gisella and Silas's story in
Princess's Forbidden Holiday Fling

All available now!

Dear Reader,

I can't believe this is the final Princesses of Rydiania book. This family was so much fun to write about. I'm so sad to see them go.

Sometimes you want something that seems out of your reach and by some magical twist of fate, your wish comes true. However, you find that what you wanted turns out to be something other than what you imagined. This is what happens for my heroine, who's on the cusp of becoming queen. And worse yet, *The Duchess Tales* gossip site is reporting her every misstep.

With snowflakes falling over New York City, Princess Gisella and Silas Cabot meet. Their goal is to create the first international Bee Global gala. She needs it to prove to herself and others that she is capable of being queen. He needs the event to be spectacular in order to expand his PR empire.

The one thing they aren't prepared for this very special Christmas is their growing feelings for each other. However, if they want a future together, they're going to have to fight for it. But will their love be strong enough to overcome the obstacles?

Happy reading,

Jennifer

Award-winning author **Jennifer Faye** pens fun contemporary romances. Internationally published with books translated into more than a dozen languages, she is a two-time winner of the *RT Book Reviews* Reviewers' Choice Award and winner of the CataRomance Reviewers' Choice Award. Now living her dream, she resides with her very patient husband and Writer Kitty. When she's not plotting out her next romance, you can find her with a mug of tea and a book. Learn more at jenniferfaye.com.

Books by Jennifer Faye

Harlequin Romance

Princesses of Rydiania

His Accidentally Pregnant Princess
Royal Mom for the Duke's Daughter

Greek Paradise Escape

Greek Heir to Claim Her Heart
It Started with a Royal Kiss
Second Chance with the Bridesmaid

Wedding Bells at Lake Como

Bound by a Ring and a Secret
Falling for Her Convenient Groom

Visit the Author Profile page
at Harlequin.com for more titles.

Praise for
Jennifer Faye

"A fantastic romantic read that is a joy to read from start to finish, *The CEO, the Puppy and Me* is another winner by the immensely talented Jennifer Faye."
—*Goodreads*

CHAPTER ONE

Almost a queen...

The words echoed in her mind.

Her Royal Highness the Crown Princess of Rydiania frowned as she stared out the tall windows on the thirty-eighth floor of a Manhattan office building. Lights shimmered across the darkening horizon. A gentle snow continued to fall upon the city, softening the sharp lines and hiding the blemishes.

Her gaze moved to Rockefeller Center and the giant Christmas tree that lit up the evening. The colorful twinkling lights glowed in the night. The scene appeared as though it were taken from the front of a Christmas card.

With it being December, it was already dark at four fifty-four in the afternoon. And the tree's multicolored lights filled the winter evening with an array of festive colors. As Princess Gisella stared at the tree, she couldn't help but think of the holiday activities going on at the palace. A gentle sigh escaped her lips.

Her mother, the Queen, would be overseeing the placement of the royal Christmas tree. It would be placed in the foyer with its upper branches soaring up to the second floor. It was always a magnificent sight to behold. All the while, the King would make himself scarce while the decorating took place. A smile tugged at her lips. Her father was never one for all of the fuss that went into decorating.

This would be the first holiday season that all of her siblings were living away from the palace. Even she was abroad taking care of palace business. She had never been away from home at Christmastime and though she wouldn't admit it to anyone, she was a bit homesick.

Earlier that year, her brother, Prince Istvan, had stepped down as heir to the throne to marry the woman of his dreams. It left Gisella stepping into the role of Rydiania's future queen. She'd always believed she was the right person to be heir to the crown. She'd just never thought it would actually become reality.

Everything had happened in rapid succession, starting with her father's Parkinson's diagnosis to her brother stepping away from the throne. She was scrambling to get up to speed with everything her life would now entail as queen.

It was quite an undertaking to move from the spare heir to the crown princess.

And not only that but now she was expected to marry. It wasn't a requirement of becoming queen, but her parents and the privy council thought it would give her position as queen the appearance of a more mature, wiser ruler. She didn't know that she agreed with that, but she was overruled. The kingdom's charter specified she had to marry someone of royal lineage. And her mother had already negotiated the "perfect" husband for her. On New Year's Day the announcement of her engagement to Prince Matis from a small island kingdom in the Mediterranean would be made official. The thought left an uneasy feeling in the pit of her stomach.

She shifted her thoughts to her mission: to oversee the preparations for the first international Bee Global gala. This trip was like an unofficial test to prove to the King and the royal privy council, as well as the kingdom, that she was the right future leader. In order to achieve that level of confidence, nothing about this trip could go wrong.

"Your Highness?"

Gisella turned to her personal assistant, Stephanie. "Has Mr. Cabot arrived?"

She shook her head. "Uh…no, ma'am."

Nothing could go wrong. Nothing at all. And

yet this was to be her first in-person meeting with Mr. Cabot and he was a no-show.

"Where is he?" She struggled to keep her rising frustration under control. "Doesn't he understand how important this meeting is?"

"I don't know, Your Highness."

"Then what is it?"

"You wanted to be notified if there were any new postings about the royal family." Her assistant's face was void of emotion.

Stephanie didn't normally work as her secretary, but with the holidays, Gisella had given some of her staff with young families the opportunity to remain in Rydiania. Stephanie was an assistant in the Princess's office, but Gisella's usual secretary saw promise in the young woman and recommended that Stephanie be given greater responsibility.

Gisella hadn't made up her mind about Stephanie. She was easily flustered and always appeared to be on her phone, but so far, she'd completed her tasks satisfactorily.

Gisella hoped the news about her family was positive. "Is it about the gala?"

Stephanie glanced down at the ground. "In a way."

Gisella didn't like cryptic answers. They usually preceded something bad. After the hatchet job a gossip site did before her brother's wedding, her family was due some positive coverage.

Gisella crossed her arms. "Where is this news?"

"It… It's a post on *Duchess Tales*."

Hope fled her. The chance of *The Duchess Tales* printing something positive about her family was slim to none. Gisella schooled her features so as not to reveal her inner frustration.

The popular site was well known in Rydiania. It claimed to be the number one spot for all royal news. They posted at all hours of the day or night with "breaking" news. They gave the appearance of having sources planted everywhere. It amazed her the amount of information they were able to gather and at such great speed. Even more worrisome was how they were able to post news about the royal family even before all of her family members were notified of the matter.

"How is it possible that no one has been able to reveal the person behind that terrible gossip site?" She couldn't help but think of the way the site and its lies had nearly destroyed her brother's wedding. The anguish it had caused her family was reprehensible.

"I don't know what to say. The palace has looked into *The Duchess Tales*, but they don't have a physical office they could find. They couldn't even find a dedicated phone line. It would appear the Duchess uses burner phones. They are very good." Stephanie sounded quite impressed.

"There's nothing good about them!" Gisella hadn't meant to lose her temper. She watched as her assistant's eyes momentarily widened. She hadn't meant for the words to be so emphatic, but she was so tired of the troublesome site. "How is that possible? How do their sources reach them if their location and phone number are constantly changing?"

"I don't know, ma'am." The young woman shrugged. "Is there anything else I can do for you?"

Gisella shook her head as she reached for her phone. At least it would keep her from thinking how late Mr. Cabot was and how her patience was wearing razor thin.

She pulled up the website and right at the top of the site was the post her assistant had pointed out:

TO BE CROWNED OR NOT?

Gisella's back teeth ground together. What was it with this Duchess person? Why were they always out to stir up trouble for her family?

It appeared now that all of her siblings had

found true love and were in committed relationships that it was her turn to be dragged over the coals. She should just close the page without even reading the article. But she knew in her position as crown princess that she wasn't afforded the luxury of sticking her head in the sand. She had to see what was being said about her and do her best to offset the bad coverage.

This Christmas it appears the Rydianian palace is deserted. All of the King and Queen's grown children are spending the holiday season elsewhere. Even the Crown Princess has decided to spend the season abroad.

Of course, it's said that she's in New York to host the annual Bee Global gala. But I can't help but wonder if there's more to this trip. After all, it's rumored that she and the King are at odds. The Princess is said to be very headstrong and unwilling to follow directions from the palace.

Is this why she had to leave so far in advance of the gala? Is there trouble at the palace? Is her chance of being crowned queen in jeopardy?

Keep reading, my lovely watchers, as I will share the details as they unfold.
xox, Duchess

Those were bold lies. Her stomach knotted into a tight ball. Why did the Duchess have to keep stirring the pot where the royal family was concerned? Why did they have to dream up trouble where none existed? Gisella's back teeth ground together as she placed her phone in her purse.

She got to her feet and began to pace in front of the window. *The Duchess Tales* was undermining her efforts to gain her kingdom's trust. This was bad. So bad.

This gala had to be a work of perfection. She had to prove the naysayers wrong, including *The Duchess Tales*. She was the right leader for the kingdom. She would show them all.

"May I get you anything?"

The friendly voice drew Gisella's attention. She turned to find Mr. Cabot's administrative assistant with silver bobbed hair, black-rimmed glasses and a worried look. "Yes. You could produce Mr. Cabot." She checked the time. "He's more than twenty minutes late."

"He's on his way." Mrs. Anderson forced a small smile. "He should be here soon."

Soon wasn't the answer she wanted. "When exactly is soon?"

"I… I expect him any moment." Mrs. Anderson started toward the door before turning back to her. "This isn't like him. Mr. Cabot is normally very punctual." The woman left her alone in the office with her thoughts.

Gisella perched on the edge of the large black leather chair behind the large cherrywood desk. Her shoulders were tense. A headache started to pulsate in her temples.

She attempted to distract herself by gazing around the office. The most impressive part was the wall of windows behind her. Being on the thirty-eighth floor, they gave an impressive view of Manhattan.

On two of the walls was a collection of black-and-white prints of various sights around the city. They were impressive shots. But it was the built-in bookcases that garnered her attention.

She stood and went to investigate. She liked to know as much as she could about a person she would be working closely with. And so far, the only things she knew about Mr. Cabot were what had been written on his website.

She'd suspected that he would read fiction novels, but to her great surprise, she found most of the titles on the shelves were biographies. *Intriguing.* There were some reference books. And finally at the bottom of one shelf she found some paperback novels. All of them appeared to be fantasy books. As she took a closer look, she realized that none of the spines were creased. He was either a very careful reader or he'd never opened the books. *Even more intriguing.*

After making her way around the office, she

returned to the black leather chair behind the desk. She sat back and crossed her legs. *Where is he?* Her foot rapidly tapped the air.

Her French-manicured fingertips drummed on the armrest. She was not accustomed to being kept waiting. This project was too important.

In the outer office she overheard Mrs. Anderson say, "Is everything all right?"

"Yes. I'm sorry for keeping you."

"Sir, my granddaughter's Christmas program is this evening and she's an elf in the play."

"Oh, yes. I didn't mean to hold you up. I'll see you tomorrow."

Gisella took in the man's disheveled appearance. He was tall. His brown hair was scattered, like he'd been running his fingers through it numerous times. There was a smudge of dirt on his cheek. She found that quite strange. He also wasn't wearing a coat and it was snowing outside.

Dark brows framed his eyes while lines of exhaustion marred his face as though he'd had a hard day. There was a part of her that felt bad for him, but the crown princess part of her expected more from him with the large amount of money she was paying him.

His dark gray suit jacket was wrinkled, like he'd been sleeping in it. His blue dress shirt's top buttons were undone and his tie was missing. She had to wonder if this was his normal appearance. If so, she wasn't impressed.

Oh, sure, he was handsome. Very handsome indeed. But she hadn't hired him for his looks. His stellar reputation for pulling off the most-talked-about events in New York was what had led her to hiring him.

They'd never met in person. They'd had a few video chats and phone calls as they'd worked through setting up the details for the upcoming event, which would host foreign dignitaries as well as scientists who would be awarded grants to continue their work in helping to sustain and grow the bee colonies not only in Rydiania but throughout the world.

Mr. Cabot approached her. "Your Majesty."

He bowed. When he raised his head, their gazes met. She noticed how his eyes were blue like a cloudless summer morning. They were bottomless as though she could get lost in them. But there was something else about them—a troubled look. Before she could determine anything, he blinked and it was like a wall had gone up between them.

"Mr. Cabot—"

"Call me Silas."

Perhaps in another situation she would take the liberty, but these weren't friendly circumstances. "Mr. Cabot, you are very late." She sent him a pointed stare. "I have to be going. I have a dinner meeting to attend."

"I apologize for my delay." He hesitated. "It was unavoidable."

She waited for him to explain his delay, but he said nothing further. It surprised her. She thought he would be groveling to fix things. It made her wonder if there had been some sort of emergency or if he'd just plain forgotten about their meeting. The latter thought didn't sit well with her.

Her gaze met his unwavering stare. He didn't appear the least bit contrite. He acted as though his actions wouldn't have consequences.

She needed someone who took the event as seriously as she did. "I'm sure whatever excuse you have is legitimate, but I need someone that makes my event their priority."

His shoulders straightened. "It is my priority."

"I need someone who is prompt."

"It won't happen again." His tone was firm.

There was a part of her that wanted to believe him, but this wasn't just about her. There was her kingdom that was counting on her to get this right. She had elevated her small kingdom onto the global stage. Everyone would be watching her and the televised awards ceremony. There was no room to take chances with someone who was obviously displaying poor judgment.

Her stomach hurt as her headache persisted. She couldn't just ignore his tardiness. Something like this could ruin the plans for the gala. The thought was unacceptable. If he couldn't take his commitments seriously, she couldn't work with him.

She put on her coat before turning back to him. "I don't see this working out." The words passed by her lips before she registered their enormity. "It's best we end our arrangement now. My people will forward you the remainder of your payment."

She moved past him and smelled smoke. What in the world? She was curious about where he'd been. *A bonfire?* But it was none of her business and it wouldn't sway her decision.

When she reached the doorway, Mr. Cabot said, "The event is in less than two weeks. You won't be able to find someone available at this time of the year to step in at the last minute. Stay and we can work this out."

His words reinforced her own worry. It wouldn't be easy to find a replacement and the holidays would definitely complicate matters. But she was the Crown Princess. People would be eager to be on an international stage with her. And she wasn't about to let this man see her as indecisive.

She glanced over her shoulder. "That's my problem. I really must be going. Good evening."

His eyes darkened. He was mad at her? If he cared that much, he wouldn't have been late. His lack of explanation left her to assume that he didn't have a good excuse. She exited to the outer office, where her security detail awaited her.

She could feel Silas Cabot's gaze following her. There was a part of her that expected him to follow her to the elevator and beg for another chance, but he didn't do that. He was either a very proud man or a very foolish one. She wasn't sure in this case that they were much different.

Definitely not his best first meeting.

Silas Cabot's hands clenched at his sides. He coughed. His throat burned. Since when were his office lights so bright? His head pounded like a big bass drum. He pressed his fingertips to his temples.

He moved to his desk chair that the Princess had just vacated. He dropped onto it. In that moment, it felt as though the pressure of the world was weighing on him.

His first in-person meeting with the Princess had been an utter disaster—a disaster of the most significant proportion. If his head would stop hurting, he would figure out how to fix this situation. He yanked open his desk drawer and removed a bottle of painkillers. With two white pills in his palm, he moved to the little fridge and retrieved a bottle of water.

After he downed the pills, he returned to his desk. He wasn't used to being dismissed. People constantly vied for him to take on their account. He only took the cream of the crop.

And being fired by the Princess of Rydiania was going to cripple his company. Once word got out, and it would get out, his company would crumble. No amount of explanations would undo this damage. The people he dealt with cared more about appearances than the truth.

Worst of all, the merger he'd been working on for the past year would fall apart. He couldn't let that happen. He couldn't let some spoiled princess destroy his life's work—a woman who clearly thought someone else would pick up the pieces for her.

The truth of the matter was he had been on his way back to the office after stopping at his mother's house with plenty of time to spare. He'd asked his driver to stop for an afternoon coffee. And that's when his plans had begun to unravel.

He stopped his mind from returning to that chilling memory.

Things had certainly gone awry, but it didn't mean they couldn't be righted. There wasn't a chance he was giving up on the royal account. This was just a small setback. It could be remedied.

He had to do something he wasn't accustomed to doing—he had to grovel. Just the thought rubbed him the wrong way. He should have anticipated something like this when he'd taken on a princess as a client.

Before he changed his mind, he sat down at his desk. "Gladys."

When his assistant didn't appear at the doorway, he recalled that she'd left for the day. If only his head would quit hurting, he could think clearly. Another bout of coughing overtook him.

After a quick internet search, he found one of the florists he used for business purposes. He called and found the shop was closed. He tried another. It too was closed. On the third try, he reached a florist that was open.

"This is Silas Cabot. I need a bouquet delivered."

"Yes, sir. What day do you need them there?"

"Today."

"Sir, I'm sorry but we're closing for the evening."

Silas cleared his throat. "I'll make it worth your time."

"But my driver is gone for the day."

"What about first thing in the morning? The earlier, the better." Silas mentioned a large amount of money as an incentive. "Will that make it possible?"

"Yes, sir. I'll see to it personally."

Silas took great pains in picking out just the right arrangement and then he had a card added. Flowers were a good start, but he knew there had to be something more—something to make his peace offering stand out. He gave it some more thought.

CHAPTER TWO

Decisions must be made.

Early the next morning, Gisella was wide awake and dressed. She hadn't slept much the night before. She mentally berated herself for acting rashly by firing Mr. Cabot. So much was riding on this event. It was her very first time on a global stage.

This gala would set the tone for her reign. It had to be calm, organized and timely. So far none of those adjectives could be associated with Mr. Silas Cabot. And yet his warning echoed in her mind about not being able to replace him at the last moment.

Instead of sleeping, she'd spent much of the night staring into the darkness, thinking of all the final details still to be dealt with. How could Mr. Cabot have fooled her all of this time? During each of their video meetings he'd made it seem as though everything was on track. Of course, those meetings had been very brief and to the point. He'd always been in a rush as though he did everything at his company himself. But she knew that wasn't the truth because she'd had his company fully vetted before she hired him. His company had more than six hundred employees so why was he always in such a rush?

And yet he gave the impression that he had everything under control. However, now that she'd met him in person, it was as if everything she thought she knew about this professional man had been nothing more than a charade.

And then there was his disheveled appearance. What in the world had he been up to before he arrived at their meeting?

Not having time to waste, she pushed aside her thoughts of Mr. Cabot. She stepped out of her bedroom into the living area of the spacious suite. She'd been accompanied on this trip by not only her security detail but also a slimmed-down staff that included her personal secretary and a couple of aides. When you were famous it was hard to do some things for yourself that other people took for granted—like running out for a coffee or picking up essentials at a store.

She said good morning to everyone. She made her way to the table for a croissant when she noticed a large bouquet of flowers in shades of white and red with green trimmings. It was beautiful and festive. It was very thoughtful of the hotel.

And then she noticed a couple of felt bees popping up in the arrangement. They were adorable and drew her in for a closer look. It was then she noticed a small card between the blooms.

She plucked the card from the arrangement. It read:

My deepest apologies. It won't happen again.
Silas

She continued to stare at the card. Was it possible she'd overreacted to his being late for their meeting? She didn't think so. She hadn't misconstrued his tardiness.

But would it behoove her to give Mr. Cabot another chance? After all, he knew all of the details of the event. If she were to hire someone else, it would take a lot of time to bring the new firm up to date.

Her gaze moved back to the flowers and the cute bees. She appreciated his attention to detail. It was one of the reasons she'd hired his company.

Not having time to dwell over her decision, she said, "Stephanie, please call Mr. Cabot's office and let them know I'd like to meet with him this morning. Make it as soon as possible."

Stephanie nodded. "Yes, Your Highness."

In no time, the meeting was set. Gisella hoped she wasn't making a mistake by giving the man a second chance. She wished she had someone to confer with, but this was all on her.

On the ride to Mr. Cabot's office, she took a call from the King. "How are things going?" her father asked. "Is everything on track for the gala?"

She recalled her meeting last night with Mr. Cabot and quickly dismissed it. "Yes. Everything is going smoothly."

"I hear a note of hesitation in your voice. What's the matter?"

Her stomach knotted. She swallowed hard and hoped when she spoke that her voice didn't betray her worry. "I'm sorry. I'm a bit distracted. It's snowing here."

"And that's all?"

"Yes. Traffic is backed up and I don't want to be late." Like Mr. Cabot had been for their meeting last evening.

They talked for a few more minutes before she disconnected the call. She checked the messages on her phone before her car pulled to a stop in front of the office building that housed SC Public Relations.

Her door was opened and she stepped onto the sidewalk. The snow was coming down so fast now that the sidewalk was white. Gisella snuggled deeper into her black wool coat with a red scarf.

She took two steps forward when a crowd of reporters descended upon her. She inwardly groaned as outwardly she smiled. She couldn't believe Mr. Cabot had leaked it to the press that she would be here this morning. This was it. She wasn't rehiring him. She didn't care how good-looking he was or how pretty the flowers were that he'd sent her. This was going to be her line in the sand.

A reporter held out a microphone. "Your Highness, are you going to see Silas Cabot?"

She could deny it, but what would be the point? It was no secret that Mr. Cabot's firm was working on her event. She swallowed hard. "Yes, I am." She kept moving. "Please excuse me."

"What do you think about him being a hero?"

Surely she hadn't heard the reporter correctly, but she didn't have time to question the man as her security team ushered her safely inside the building. All the while she wondered what the reporter was talking about. She pondered whether Mr. Cabot would mention it at their meeting. She hoped so. She was curious to know what he'd done to earn the moniker of hero.

She rode the elevator to the thirty-eighth floor.

When she reached the office, she was immediately ushered into Mr. Cabot's inner office, where he was sitting behind his large desk.

When he lifted his head and their gazes met, a smile lifted the corners of his mouth. Her heart skipped a beat. She averted her gaze, taking in the modern-style office, even though she'd had plenty of time to admire the furnishings the prior evening.

When she stopped in front of his desk, her gaze returned to him. This time instead of looking disheveled, he looked like he'd just stepped off the cover of some magazine with his short hair perfectly styled. Her fingers tingled with the desire to reach out and run through the dark strands. He was clean-shaven. There was nothing amiss with his appearance.

He got to his feet. "Good morning, Your Royal Highness."

"Good morning."

"Please have a seat." He gestured to the leather armchairs in front of his desk. Once she was seated, he sat down. "Thank you for agreeing to meet with me again."

She placed her purse between herself and the arm of the chair. When her gaze met his again, she was immediately struck by the intensity of his gaze. She refused to glance away and let him know that he affected her in any way.

"I must admit that I was against coming back here." It was the truth.

"If I may ask, what changed your mind?"

She debated on what she should tell him. She didn't want to give him too much information—for him to think that his ploy would work on her again. But she supposed it wouldn't hurt to tell him.

"I was impressed with your attention to detail with the flower arrangement."

He smiled. "You liked that, huh?"

She was quiet for a moment. "My coming here doesn't mean everything is back on track. I can't work with someone who isn't reliable."

She expected him to excuse his actions the prior day with his heroic action. It bothered her when people searched for excuses instead of just owning their actions. She sat there trying to make up her mind about this man.

"I have lined up a number of items for the event that need your final approval. We can do a walk-through of the site for the party. And then we can go over some of the finer details."

As he continued to lay out his agenda for the day, she didn't know if she should be impressed that he wasn't trying to excuse their first meeting or be frustrated that he acted as though nothing had happened.

"Before we do any of that we need to talk."

He leaned back in his chair. "Certainly. What would you like to talk about?"

She struggled not to sigh in frustration. He certainly wasn't making this easy on her. "I would like to understand what happened yesterday. I made it clear before I arrived that my time was limited and that we couldn't waste any of it. And that's why I need the person working with me to be as dedicated to this project as I am." And to drive home her seriousness, she said, "I'm not sure you're that person."

He sat forward, resting his elbows on his dark desk. She'd gained his full attention. *Good*. He needed to know just how important this event was for her.

He laced his fingers together. "What happened yesterday will never happen again."

Once more with the evasiveness. She didn't like it. "Perhaps we should just leave things here. I'll have my staff take over the remainder of the planning."

"Wait. You can't just walk away."

Was he kidding? Did he not know that she was a princess, soon to be a queen? There was very little she couldn't do.

"I can. And I am." She got to her feet.

He let out a frustrated sigh. "Don't go."

Her gaze met his. Neither of them blinked as though they were battling for control. She could tell that he wasn't used to taking orders. He either opened up to her or she intended to walk out the door.

"Please sit down." He gestured to the chair across from him. "I'll tell you whatever it is you need to know."

For a long moment, she didn't move. She didn't want him to get the impression that she was easily swayed. Feeling as though she'd finally gotten through to him that she wouldn't stand for anything to interfere with this event, she perched on the edge of the chair with her purse in her hands. If she didn't like what she heard, she was making a quick exit.

CHAPTER THREE

His body tensed.

Silas didn't like being pushed around by anyone—not even a beautiful princess. He was the boss of his flourishing company. He didn't answer to anyone and now Princess Gisella sat staring expectantly at him—waiting for him to justify being late for their prior meeting. His natural reaction was to remain silent and let her come to her own conclusions.

And yet he needed this gala to be a stunning success. If it were to fall apart now, it would cripple his company. He couldn't let that happen. He'd devoted his life to this company— making it the biggest and the best.

When he was a kid, he'd escaped his parents' arguments by losing himself inside a fantasy novel. He would devour the books one after the other.

As he grew older, his reading slipped away as he spent the bulk of his time building an empire. There wasn't time for anything else—not pleasure reading or a serious relationship. It was work from the time he woke up until late in the evening. His business had to be the biggest and the best. And now his efforts were paying off.

In the end, the professional world he operated within could be a small one, even if it spanned the globe. People in his profession kept their ears to the ground. They knew which big names were working with what PR agency. By now, they all knew the Rydiania Palace had hired his firm for this big venture.

In his mind, he could still hear the echo of his father saying: *"You're nothing but a failure."* Silas had tried everything as a child to impress his father. Nothing was ever good enough. In school, if he got all top marks except for one subject, his father focused on the lower mark. It was always like that with him. His father zeroed in on any vulnerability and used it against Silas.

While in college, his father would compare him with his father's assistant, who quickly rose through the ranks of his father's insurance agency. His father wouldn't even consider giving Silas a job. His father always had an excuse, like the work would be too hard for Silas—even though he had always been a hard worker. Or his father would claim the position took math skills—Silas always excelled in his math classes. There was just no pleasing the man. Not ever.

Silas gave himself a mental shake. He refused to let the unwelcome memories intrude upon this moment.

He cleared his throat. "I was planning to be in the office yesterday when…" He hesitated. He didn't feel the need to divulge all of the details of his life, like the fact that his mother had called in a panic because it was snowing out and she had run out of her medication. "I was called away from the office."

"I take it this was something important."

He thought of his mother and her various medical conditions, but the Princess didn't need to know those details. "Yes, it was very important. I didn't plan to be gone long."

"And yet, you were."

He pressed his lips together to keep from sighing. "Is this your story or mine?"

Her eyes momentarily widened. It didn't appear she was used to being called out. He waited until she settled back on the chair before he continued.

"After my business was concluded, I requested a car. It was a quiet afternoon in a residential area where most of the residents were still at work. And the snowstorm had just started." He stopped talking. Why was he telling her all of these details? He just needed to get to the point. "I had the driver stop at a nearby coffee shop. When I was headed back to the car, I spotted smoke. It was more than you would expect from a fireplace. And it was black."

The image was vivid in his mind. As he relayed the story, he could feel himself being back there with the snowflakes falling all around him. The street was quiet as the smell of smoke filtered through the air.

He'd looked around but there hadn't been anyone out and about except for a couple of passing cars. There was no one to make sure the family living in that house was safe.

"I ditched my coffee and ran to the house. The piercing squeal of the house's fire alarm could be heard from the street."

"You're serious?" the Princess asked. "This really happened?"

The doubt in her voice struck a nerve. His father would not believe him or would be dismissive when Silas would tell him a story. Thankfully there was his mother, who always had believed in him.

"Of course I'm serious." His words were terse. There was no point in telling her the rest if she wasn't going to believe him.

"I'm sorry. I shouldn't have said that. Please

continue." Her beautiful blue eyes implored him to continue.

He hesitated. "I ran up the steps and banged on the door. I shouted for them to get out. When I tried the door handle, it opened. The smoke rushed out." He clearly remembered stepping inside and having to squint. The smoke had burned his eyes and throat. "Suddenly a woman came rushing toward me. She was coughing and her words were rushed. But it was the look of fear in her eyes that held my attention. She begged me to rescue her baby. I told her to go outside and call 911. I pulled my overcoat up over my mouth and made my way up the stairs. The smoke was so heavy that I ended up on my knees, crawling down the hallway. All the while I was praying I'd reach the baby in time. It felt like it took forever. At last, I found the baby." He sucked in an unsteady breath as the memories kept washing over him. "With the baby tucked inside my coat, I moved as fast as I could through the house, down the steps and outside."

It had been the most horrific event he'd ever endured. The woman had been out in the snow in nothing more than jeans and a T-shirt so he'd wrapped his wool overcoat over her and the baby as they waited for help to arrive. Shortly after the fire department and medics were on the scene, he'd had his driver to take him to the office. If he had to do it all over again, he would do exactly the same thing.

The princess's mouth gaped. It took her a moment to regain her composure. "I can't believe you walked into a burning building."

"I didn't have a choice."

"You always have a choice. You chose to put their needs ahead of your own. The reporters downstairs are one hundred percent correct. You're the very definition of a hero."

He shook his head. "I did what anyone would do."

"Not everyone would risk their life for a stranger." She reached for her phone.

"What are you doing?" he asked.

She held up a finger as she stared at her phone. "It's here."

"What's here?"

"Your picture." She turned her phone around for him to see himself with the baby in his arms. "What the paper might not tell you is that the baby had to be rushed to the hospital for smoke inhalation."

The Princess's eyes filled with worry. "How is the baby now?"

"I don't know. I tried to call this morning but the hospital wouldn't give out any information."

"Maybe you should go there."

He shook his head. "I did all I could. Now I need to be here."

A look of realization came over her. "Because of me?"

He didn't confirm it. He hoped at last he'd sufficiently convinced her that he hadn't forgotten their meeting yesterday.

"Are you sure you should be working today?" The Princess studied him.

"I'm fine." Mostly fine. His throat was still a bit sore from the smoke inhalation, but the paramedics had checked him out. They said his oxygen level was fine, but he should go to the hospital to be fully checked out. He'd signed a waiver of treatment and headed directly to his office.

"I'm sorry you went through all of that, but thankfully you were in the right place at the right time."

"Anyway, we should get started." He paused. "That is if you're still willing to work with me."

"Of course I am." At last, she smiled at him.

As her lush lips lifted at the corners, it eased the worry lines on her face. She was more breathtaking in person than she was in the thousands of photos of her on the internet. Not that he'd been checking her out on the internet. It was all for business reasons and nothing more.

He liked her long, loose curls. Her golden-brown hair hung down to the middle of her back. He wondered if it was as soft and silky as it looked.

"Where shall we start today?" Her voice drew him from his rambling thoughts.

He cleared his throat. "We should go to the Metropolitan Museum of Art. I have a number of things that need to be finalized."

She nodded in agreement. "Let's go. My car is downstairs."

He stood and retrieved his coat as well as his digital notebook. He made sure to have everything digitized so it would be convenient for when he was on the go.

He turned to find the Princess was already in the outer office. As he strode to the door, he had to admit that he was surprised by the Princess. He got a glimpse of the woman beneath the serious royal persona. He hoped he'd get to see more of the woman behind the crown.

So he was a legitimate hero.

Gisella decided that this was a quality she liked in her PR person. It was good to know that he wasn't only worried about himself. The fact he'd called the hospital to check on the baby that morning said a lot about him. And so she decided a quick stop on the way to the party venue was in order.

When the car pulled to a stop in front of the hospital, Silas glanced up from his phone. "What are we doing here?"

"I thought it would be nice to check in on the little girl you rescued."

His eyes registered his surprise. "Oh. Okay. But what about your schedule?"

"Don't worry. We'll make this work."

However, her security detail was not at all delighted by the detour. They liked to do a walk-through and a threat assessment before she visited places. And though she didn't like being put on a short leash, she adhered to it most of the time. However, this wasn't one of those times. A compromise would have to be made.

The car pulled to a stop outside the hospital's main entrance. Security had them wait for a few minutes while they did a quick walk-through. Suddenly the silence in the vehicle became quite noticeable.

She should say something but she couldn't think of anything to say. Silas had been staring at his phone for the entire ride. She wondered what had him so distracted. Was it work? Or perhaps it was the headlines about his heroic rescue.

She turned to him. "Is there something you need to share?" When he glanced up with a confused look on his face, she said, "You've been engrossed with your phone the whole ride here."

He gave a quick shake of his head. "It's nothing to concern you. I was just going over some emails regarding the gala. Everything is on track."

"Good." She leaned back in the seat. "We should stop at the gift shop on the way to the little girl's room."

"I… I don't know."

She smiled. "Don't worry. I'll pick something out."

"Are you sure you want to do that?"

"Of course. I was a little girl at one point. I think I can pick out a toy for her. Unless you're opposed to the idea."

He shook his head. "Not at all."

Just then the car door swung open. They were ushered inside. Heads turned in her direction. She was used to it. It happened everywhere she went. Now that she was next in line for the throne, media attention had been all over her. But with Silas's face in the news, it might be him they'd noticed. Today they made quite the striking couple. Not *that* kind of romantic couple. She stifled a groan of frustration.

Outwardly she put on a show of smiling at the people who'd stopped and waved to her. Some had their cell phones out taking photos. She didn't stop for any selfies. They had a schedule to keep and this detour was already going to put them behind.

After stopping by the information desk and getting the little girl's room number, they moved on to the gift shop. She picked out a pink teddy bear for the little girl. And for the mother, she selected some magazines. She couldn't imagine how hard it must be for the mother to sit next to her little girl's bed. She needed a distraction and flipping the pages of a magazine would give her something to do.

Gisella noticed that Silas was quiet in the gift shop and as they rode the elevator to the pediatrics floor. A nurse's aide met them at the elevator. It appeared the staff had been alerted that they were on their way up.

Before they stepped off the elevator, Gisella held out the teddy bear to him. "Here."

His eyes widened as he looked at the teddy bear as though it were a snake about to bite him. "You give it to her."

What is it about men getting uncomfortable around babies?

Not about to take no for an answer, she pushed the teddy bear to his chest. "I'm not the hero in this story. You are."

When she let go of the stuffed animal, he caught it. And then he gestured for her to exit the elevator ahead of him. It was on this floor that she paused for selfies. How could she not? It was so sad to see all of these sweet children in hospital beds. And even though it further delayed their schedule, she smiled and chatted with the parents while Silas made his way to visit the little girl that he'd rescued from the fire.

She caught up with Silas in time to see the child's mother hand him the baby. The little one's name was Susie and her mother's name was Mary. The baby couldn't have been cuter with her chubby, rosy cheeks and golden curls. Gisella couldn't help but smile at the sight. Silas's face was tense and his shoulders rigid as though he was afraid of dropping the baby.

But as Mary talked to him and the baby blew bubbles, Gisella saw him relax. She hardly knew him and yet she knew that someday in the not-so-distant future he would make an excellent father and husband. The thought caused an uncomfortable sensation to come over her, but before she could analyze it, Silas turned to her and smiled.

It was the first time she'd seen him smile and she had to admit he was good-looking with his brooding expression, but with a smile lifting the corners of his lips, he was downright irresistible. Her heart beat faster as she smiled back at him.

When he lowered his gaze to Susie, who was starting to fuss, it was like the sun's rays had gotten lost behind a big dark cloud. The smile fell from her face. What in the world was that all about?

Even before she was the heir to the throne, it was made known to her that it was her responsibility to make a proper match when she married. There was no room in a royal's life for love and romance. Although her youngest sister, Cecelia, didn't follow royal protocol when she found her love match in the South of France. But Cecelia could afford those sorts of luxuries. Her youngest sister had always gotten away with more than Gisella had even imagined trying to do.

Gisella reassured herself that she'd done the right thing by following the rules and missing out on all of the fun that her siblings had enjoyed. She didn't know why she'd been born a serious child—at least that's what her mother had said.

Perhaps it was the calm and comfort of a regimented life that she liked so much. But as she watched Silas, she couldn't help but wonder what it'd be like to be more adventurous.

Buzz.

She retrieved her phone from her purse to find a message from her personal assistant. If they didn't get moving there was no way they'd get their schedule back on track.

She stepped forward. After a quick conversation with the very grateful mother and a photo of them all together, Gisella said, "I hate to do this but we must be going."

Silas's dark eyes momentarily widened as though he was shocked that he'd actually forgotten about their agenda for the day. Something told her he wasn't used to getting distracted from his work. Maybe they were more alike than she'd first thought.

He turned back to the young mother. "She's right. I'm happy things are going well for you both. And I'll be in touch about the crowdfunding campaign."

"Thank you so much." With the baby in one arm, the mother leaned forward with her other arm and hugged Silas.

On the way to the car, Gisella couldn't resist asking, "What was that about a crowdfunding campaign?"

"She lost everything in the fire and I said I would work on a fundraiser for her and her little girl. In the meantime, I'm going to put them up in a hotel until they're able to find a new place to live."

Gisella didn't think she could be any more impressed by him, but he once again surprised her. "That's very generous of you."

He shrugged off her compliment. "It's what anyone would do."

She thought of pointing out that he was wrong, but she wordlessly pressed her lips together. The woman and baby couldn't have had a better person come to their rescue. Now she had to hope he was just as impressive when it came to doing his job.

CHAPTER FOUR

THEIR WORKDAY FLEW by in a blur.

Silas was on his fourth coffee of the day by the time they'd toured The Met. The Princess had approved of the attire for the serving staff and chosen the dinnerware. The Princess was very interested in all of the details for this event, more so than any other of his clients.

He was impressed by the Princess's stamina. She hadn't even wanted to stop for lunch. She'd been determined they get their schedule back on track. He thought of mentioning that it wouldn't have been a problem if they hadn't taken the detour to the hospital, but he resisted the urge. He couldn't afford to upset her in any way. This event was already the talk of the town. His company had generated so much hype that his company's reputation was now linked to the success of the gala.

In hindsight, he'd been grateful to know that Susie and her mother would be fine and it gave him a chance to help them some more. In fact, when he returned to his penthouse, he intended to set up the crowdfunding campaign.

Gisella surprised him in many ways. She wasn't the spoiled princess he'd been expecting. It made him all the more determined to ensure she had a pleasant experience while working with him and his company.

And so, he and his assistant planned a surprise for the Princess for later that afternoon. It would hopefully put him solidly on her good side. And entertaining her might actually be more pleasurable than he'd originally thought.

It was nearing dinnertime as they worked in his conference room. They were joined by his staff that had been on the Bee Global project from the beginning as well as the Princess's staff: her assistant and two aides. They'd been going over the final details before the Princess departed for the evening.

They had one more thing to review—the program. The mock-up had just been delivered. Not only did the evening include dinner and an awards presentation, but there was to be entertainment and dancing. It would be quite an evening.

He reached out for the cream-colored program with embossed bumblebees in light shimmery yellow and black carrying a golden tiara encrusted with rubies. The Bee Global logo was done in raised print with the time and place at the bottom of the invitation. It was just as they'd discussed on one of their video chats.

He held it out to her. Gisella leaned forward and took it from him. She was quiet as she looked over the cover of the program. He couldn't tell if she approved of it or not.

The longer she remained quiet, the more concerned he became. "It's just like we'd discussed."

She didn't so much as acknowledge his words as she opened the program and read through the inner pages. He should busy himself with his email. Dozens of new emails had come in that day while he'd been out. Most of them were marked as a high priority.

And yet he was drawn to Gisella. She was nothing like he was expecting. He figured that everything would be done by others and she'd sweep in at the end to claim the credit. That wasn't the case with Gisella.

She was hardworking and detail oriented. He liked that in a person. He watched as her brows drew together. Her beautiful face filled with frown lines. *Oh, no.* That definitely wasn't good.

"Don't worry if there's a typo. We have time to get it fixed."

She shook her head. "It's more than a typo."

He leaned forward, resting his elbows on the desk. "What's the matter?"

She glanced up. Her blue gaze zeroed in on him. "It's the lineup."

He reached for the program and opened it. And then he searched his computer for the file with the lineup for the evening's entertainment. Once the file was open, he compared the two. It looked correct to him. "I don't understand. This matches the file we received."

"The band had to cancel due to medical reasons. My office notified you a couple of weeks ago."

He was certain he wouldn't forget something like that. He turned to his staff. "Who dealt with this?"

They all glanced at each other. Worried looks filled each of their faces. Then they turned puzzled looks back at him.

He couldn't drop the subject. It was important they get to the bottom of the mix-up. "Speak up. Who saw the email about the band canceling?"

"No one." Charles, SC's event manager, looked up from his laptop. "I just checked and there's no record of the email."

"How is that possible?" Princess Gisella asked.

Charles looked at her. His complexion paled as worry lines marred his face. "Perhaps it had the wrong email address." He visibly swallowed. "Or maybe it got lost in cyberspace. Sometimes that does actually happen."

Silas pulled up the royal emails. He'd kept all of them specifically for a reason such as this. His gaze scanned down over the subject lines. There was nothing that referenced the band canceling. "When would it have been sent?"

"I don't know." Gisella reached for her phone.

A moment of silence fell over them as they both searched for the mysterious email. He'd even started opening and scanning the emails. There was nothing there about the band canceling. And yet he knew even if it wasn't his team's fault, it was still a huge issue. The band was to play after the awards ceremony. They were to fill a large portion of the evening.

"I can't find it," Gisella said. "How can that be?" She turned to her assistant. "Do you know who was in charge of alerting the New York team?"

Her assistant's eyes widened with worry. "No, ma'am. I don't recall."

With only thirteen days until the Bee Global gala, the solution had to be quick. If this event was to unravel now, it would be sure to get back to the company he was interested in merging with in California. It would kill the deal as well as his chances of expanding coast to coast. And that couldn't happen because he wasn't a loser. He drove himself to always come out on top because that had been drilled into him from birth, nothing less was acceptable.

Everyone started arguing at the table. His people were claiming the email was never sent to them. And Gisella's people were yelling back that they'd notified his people. They were getting absolutely nowhere.

Silas stood. "Enough!"

Everyone stopped talking and turned to him. Even Gisella's eyes momentarily widened. He didn't mean to startle her. He just wanted the unproductive finger-pointing to stop.

Now that he had everyone's attention, he had to formulate a plan on the spot. "This is what we're going to do. My team will create a list of a dozen bands that could fill in. And the Princess's team will review the bands online. They will narrow down the list to the top two candidates. They will give the final names to the Princess and myself."

"When do you need those names?" Charles asked.

"You will need to have the list to the Princess's team by first thing in the morning." At the sound of the groaning and complaints that it wasn't possible, he said, "It is possible and it will be done."

Gisella turned to her people. "And my staff will have the top two bands to me by noon."

Her personal assistant and two aides frowned but they refrained from uttering their complaints.

He noticed that Gisella was still working on her computer. Her fingers moved rapidly over the keyboard. He wasn't sure what she was up to so he kept the meeting focused on their next steps to fix this problem.

He didn't know what bands would be available at the last minute and with it being the holidays, it wouldn't help the situation. But there was the enticement that this gala was a huge affair with big names attending and lots of publicity.

The next thing their teams began to argue over was what sort of band they should hire. One person thought it should be hip-hop because the award winners were young. Another thought it should be classical because this was a royal affair. Someone proposed jazz because it was uplifting.

He thought of intervening but he trusted his team. He was sure that when the dust settled they'd come up with the right sound for the event.

When Gisella looked as though she was going to enter the fray, he caught her eye and gave a slight shake of his head. There was a distinct frown on her face. He had to do something to distract her. It was the perfect time to put his plan in action.

He leaned over to her and whispered, "Come with me."

"Where?"

"You'll see." He stood and waited until she was next to him. While their people continued to argue about the band, they slipped away through a side door that led directly to his office. Once he closed the door, blocking out the cacophony of voices, he said, "Isn't this much better?"

Gisella frowned at him. "We should be in there."

He got the feeling she was used to micromanaging everything. "Why? Don't you trust your people?"

There was a slight pause, just long enough for him to notice. "Of course I do."

"Then let them do their jobs."

She pressed her hands to her rounded hips. "And what are we supposed to do?"

He couldn't deny that she intrigued him. In the twenty-four hours that he'd gotten to know her a little better, he was surprised to find that she was more of a workaholic than a pampered royal. Interesting.

"How about we sneak away?" He wanted to get to know her a little better.

"Sneak?" When he nodded, she said, "I'm a princess. I don't sneak anywhere. But if I were to *sneak away*, where exactly would you suggest I go?"

He couldn't help but smile. She was way too serious. "Would you like to see some more of the city?"

She arched a royal brow, reminding him of whom he was speaking to. "The sightseeing will have to wait. I really should go and answer some emails."

"You can't work all of the time." He shifted his weight from one foot to the other. "Besides, you skipped lunch today. You need something to eat."

"What are you suggesting?"

"I think we should go get some food."

"Together?"

"Yes, together." He paused, wondering if she was worried about being seen in public with him. "It can be a working dinner."

She arched a brow. "I thought we just went over everything."

"There are always details that need to be taken care of. And I know of a place, not far from here. So, what do you say?"

She didn't immediately answer. He wondered

if she was trying to find a polite way of backing out of the invitation. "Okay. Let's go. We can take my car."

"No car is necessary, if you don't mind a little walking." He glanced down to find that she was wearing a sensible pair of black boots.

"Don't look so surprised. We have snow in Rydiania." She wore a satisfied smile. "Where exactly are we going?"

"It's a surprise."

"What am I supposed to tell my security detail?"

"That they can follow us if they like."

He couldn't imagine always having to tell people of your plans. It definitely did away with the spontaneity.

She in turn told her bodyguard of their plans. What was his name? Nick? Mick? Oh, yes. It was Vic. He was surprised by the size of her security detail, but he supposed it was expected since she was soon to be a queen.

Bundled up in their warm winter coats, they headed out on their adventure. With her security close behind, they made their way up the block. Darkness had already settled over the city. He noticed Gisella taking in the white twinkling lights adorning the smallish trees that lined either side of the avenue while the store windows were trimmed with red, white and green decorations.

He didn't like that they'd already run into a problem with the gala. He honestly didn't know if his staff or hers had made the mistake with the band. Still, he didn't want it to be an issue between him and the Princess.

He cleared his throat. "I apologize."

Her head turned to him. "You don't have to apologize about the band mix-up."

He was relieved to hear that she was reasonable. It would make working closely together much easier. "I'm sure we'll be able to get it resolved quickly."

"I hope."

"Have faith." He stopped walking. "We're here."

The Princess glanced around. "Where? I don't see a restaurant."

He gestured to the hot dog cart with the large blue-and-yellow umbrella. "If you want a true New York experience, you have to have a hot dog." When she didn't immediately respond, he said, "But if you'd prefer to get out of the cold—"

"No, this is fine." The hesitancy in her voice let him know that she wasn't as confident as she wanted him to believe.

"They offer the best hot dogs in the city."

"Do you know this from personal experience?"

"Yes." When her eyes momentarily widened, he said, "What can I say? I like hot dogs. So over the years I've tried most of the vendors in this area. Lucky for me the best is near my office." He still had the feeling she wasn't enthused with the idea of getting her dinner from a street vendor. "Forget this. We'll go somewhere else."

When he went to walk away, she placed a hand on his forearm. "No. We're staying. I'm looking forward to a hot dog."

His gaze met hers. "Are you sure?"

"Positive." She glanced around. "It's definitely different. And if this is your favorite, it must be good."

They placed their order and got some food for her security team, who initially resisted his offer. However, when Gisella insisted they have something to eat, not one of those big, tough men objected.

With their hot dogs in hand, Gisella asked, "Shall we go back to the office?"

"Not yet. I have one more surprise."

"Let me guess, ice cream from another street vendor?"

"No. But if you'd like ice cream, I know of this little place not far from here. Would you like to go there?"

She smiled and shook her head. "No. I was just giving you a hard time. I'm curious to see what you have in mind. By the way, thank you."

Now he was the one who was confused. "For what?"

"Sharing your favorite place with me."

No one had ever thanked him for sharing this place with them, but then again, he'd never brought any of his dates here. Not that he was ashamed of the vendor food, but rather he was always holding his dates at arm's length.

Not that this was a date. Not even close. And maybe he hadn't thought through this dinner completely, but as he watched the Princess eat her hot dog and smile, he decided his plan to give her a New York experience was working.

Next, he told her security detail where they were going before he hailed a taxi. He wasn't about to have the Princess walk nine blocks in December.

A few minutes later, the taxi dropped them off at an entrance to Central Park. Even though it was wintertime, the city was bustling with locals and tourists alike.

"What are we doing here?" she asked.

"Come with me." He instinctively took her gloved hand in his as he led her into the park.

They stopped in front of a statue. When they turned to the road, she noticed a horse-drawn carriage parked in the road. "We're going in that?"

"If you'd like."

She smiled and nodded her consent.

Since he'd had his assistant make the reservations, they didn't have to wait for a ride. He helped her up into the carriage and then he sat next to her.

Once they were settled under the warm blankets that were provided for them, the carriage set off. He'd even made special arrangements to have a thermos of hot chocolate provided.

He didn't normally go to this personal extent to please a client, but the Princess wasn't just any client. And things had gotten off to a rocky start. But when he glanced over at her as they made their way through the park, he had a feeling things would be greatly improved at the end of this ride.

He noticed a stray snowflake that settled on her long eyelashes. His fingers tingled with the desire to swipe it away. As though she read his thoughts, she brushed it away. He felt a sense of disappointment.

He stifled a sigh. What was wrong with him? It wasn't like this was a date. It was a strategic move to entertain a client. Though he did have a stray thought that if this was an actual date it wouldn't be so bad.

The thought startled him. He couldn't let his mind continue to meander down this dangerous path. He turned his attention back to the Christmas-card-like views.

From their spot in Central Park, they could stare out at the surrounding skyscrapers that were lit up against the inky-black sky. But for him, it wasn't the pretty lights that held his attention. His attention kept returning to the gorgeous woman sitting next to him. Maybe the carriage ride hadn't been his brightest idea because it was just too cozy with her next to him while they shared the blankets.

He resisted the urge to stretch his arm and drape it over her slender shoulders. Still, he imagined drawing her close and sharing a steamy kiss on this chilly evening. Realizing the direction of his thoughts, he drew them up short.

He needed to do something to distract himself. He reached for the hot chocolate at the same time that she did. He immediately pulled his hand back. Even though they were both wearing gloves, he felt a tingly sensation in his fingers. He dismissed the moment as nothing more than a surprised reaction.

"Would you like some hot chocolate?" she offered.

He shook his head. "It's okay. You can have it."

"There's more than enough to share." She

pulled off her gloves and poured the steamy drink.

He removed his gloves so as not to spill the cocoa. When she held the cup out to him, their bare fingers touched. The sensation was like a bolt of static electricity. It zinged up his arm and settled in his chest.

Their gazes met and held a moment too long. His gaze dipped to her cheeks and petite nose, which were now pink from the cold air. His vision continued downward until he reached her rosy lips. He wondered if they were warm like her fingers or if they needed warming. He imagined leaning to the side and pressing his mouth to hers.

As though she sensed his errant thoughts, she glanced away. It was a good thing because her lips might have been too much of a temptation for him. If they'd have stared into each other's eyes a moment longer, he would have given in to his desires.

And it would have been a mistake. She was a very important client. She was pivotal to taking his company from big to bigger. He had to stay focused on the business and keeping the Princess happy. Nothing could distract him from the job at hand—not even his desire to kiss her.

In all of his planning for this outing, he hadn't thought of requesting two cups and obviously no one else had either. If he had, they wouldn't have had that awkward moment. He couldn't help but notice how intimate this whole adventure felt.

And when it was over and he was walking her to her awaiting car, it was all he could do not to kiss her goodbye. He kept reminding himself that this wasn't a date. Not a date at all.

CHAPTER FIVE

It was a lovely evening.

Though the dinner was only so-so, the carriage ride was unforgettable.

Gisella kept replaying the whole thing over and over in her mind. There had been a moment when she'd thought he was going to kiss her. Even the memory made her heart race.

She couldn't help but wonder if he took all of his dates on a carriage ride through Central Park. Not that it had been a date. He was just being nice and showing her the sights. The problem was when his dark eyes had gazed deeply into hers, she'd forgotten all about palace business and instead wondered what it'd be like to be wrapped in his muscled arms with his lips pressed to hers. The thought sent her heart once more pitter-pattering.

Not that it was ever going to happen. After all, she was the Crown Princess. She wasn't permitted any dalliances—even with the sexiest man on the planet. A disappointed sigh crossed her lips.

She'd also noticed that he wasn't willing to open up about himself, but she felt as though she'd learned a lot about him just by observing his actions. He had been thoughtful when he'd arranged for the carriage ride so she could see the Christmas lights. He was also detail oriented by arranging for the warm blankets and the hot chocolate. And he'd used self-restraint when he'd resisted kissing her. Not many men would have held back. She wondered why he hadn't gone for it. She'd wanted to ask, but she worried that somehow, she might have read the situation wrong. And she didn't want to embarrass herself.

The following afternoon Gisella sat once again in the office of SC Public Relations. As Silas talked to one of his employees, she wondered if he had a significant other. Yes, that must be it. It would explain why he hadn't kissed her. She didn't know why she hadn't thought of it before.

As quickly as she felt satisfied by solving the mystery, she suddenly felt a great sense of disappointment. With Silas already off the market, her fantasy had absolutely no chance of coming true.

It wasn't like she didn't have someone in her

life. It wasn't romantic. It was more like a pre-arranged relationship—one she honestly wasn't interested in but she knew eventually it would be her duty to commit herself to a loveless marriage because it was in the best interest of the kingdom.

"What do you think?" Silas looked directly at her.

The breath caught in her lungs. She wasn't used to being caught daydreaming when she was supposed to be working. What was it about being around this man that had her acting out of character?

She swallowed hard. "What do *you* think?"

He sent her a puzzled look but then proceeded to give his opinion about the two bands that her staff had selected. His opinion sounded reasonable so she said, "I agree. Now, how do we narrow it down?"

"We're going to listen to them and choose the best fit."

She liked that idea. "How soon?"

He checked the time on his watch. "In an hour."

Knock-knock.

All heads turned to the open doorway. An older woman stood there. She had silver hair cut in a bob that brushed her shoulders. She wore a red dress coat with a sparkly wreath pinned to the lapel. Her porcelain face was powdered and on her lips was red lipstick.

Her mouth bowed into a warm smile. "I hope I'm not interrupting."

"Mom." Silas moved toward her. "What are you doing here?"

"I had a doctor's appointment and I wanted to stop by to say hello. But I'm sorry for interrupting."

So this was Silas's mother. Interesting. Gisella's gaze moved to Silas. His cold business exterior melted into something warmer. Was that a look of caring in his eyes? So there was more to him than he wanted to let on.

He moved toward the doorway. "Mom, it's fine. Come on in."

The woman's gaze moved around the roomful of people who were all staring back at her. Her warm smile wavered.

Gisella followed him. She smiled at the woman. "It's a pleasure to meet you, Mrs. Cabot."

The woman's gaze moved to her. First her eyes widened and then her mouth dropped. "You're… You're a princess."

Gisella's smile broadened. "I am. And it's a pleasure to meet you."

Mrs. Cabot bowed her head. When she lifted it, she said, "I'm too old to curtsy. I might not be able to get back up."

Gisella nodded in understanding. "There's no need for that."

Mrs. Cabot sent her a hesitant look. "I didn't know my son would be meeting with you or I wouldn't have interrupted."

Silas reached out and touched his mother's shoulder as though to regain her attention. "Mom, is something wrong?"

She shook her head. "I… I shouldn't have come." She turned to walk away.

Silas rushed after her. "Mom, wait."

Gisella felt better about working with him. Because a man that was good to his mother was almost always a good guy.

She watched as Silas asked his mother to wait for him in the hallway. And then he returned to her. He gave her an address. "Meet me there in an hour and we'll wrap up the band issue."

"But where is this?"

"Trust me."

"But I don't even know you."

"Then this will give you a chance to know me better." He returned to his mother's side without even giving Gisella a chance to say anything.

She moved to the hallway and watched as the elevator doors opened. Silas waited for his mother to enter first and then he followed her.

Gisella stood there quietly staring as the elevator door slid shut. Silas was unlike any other man in her life. He didn't scrape and bow. Far from it. He treated her just like anyone else. And secretly she liked it.

Back at the palace, everything was done by protocol. It was Your Highness this and Your Highness that. No one but her siblings, who were now living elsewhere, really saw the woman behind the crown.

And there was the way he talked to her, like he truly valued her input, and it wasn't just because she was a princess. He could be in charge one moment and laid-back in the next. Although she noticed that he didn't talk much about himself. He enjoyed talking about his business. When he spoke of SC Public Relations, his eyes lit up and his face became animated. He definitely loved what he did for a living.

She had to admit that she was indeed intrigued by him. She gave the address to her security detail and an hour later, she was in another elevator riding up to the top floor.

She approached Penthouse #1 and knocked.

When the door swung open, Silas stood there. His tie was gone and the top buttons of his dress shirt had been undone.

He opened the door fully. "Come in."

Her bodyguard Vic halted her. He insisted on doing a sweep of the residence. Silas consented.

It was awkward but Silas seemed to understand the necessity.

A few moments later, Vic cleared the penthouse. She turned to her bodyguards. "Stay here." Each of her two bodyguards took up their position on either side of the door. And then she stepped inside the spacious apartment with high ceilings.

"Welcome. Let me take your coat." He held out his hand.

She shrugged out of her red coat and handed it to him. "Thank you."

"Can I get you something to drink?"

"Some white wine if you have it."

"Coming up."

"Is this your place?" She glanced around at the black leather couches and all of the modern touches.

"It is."

The walls were a light gray and the lighting was soft, but it was the view that drew her to the tall windows. This is what she'd miss most when she returned to Rydiania. She loved the city at night. With the twinkling of lights, it was a magical place. There was a vibrancy here that she'd never felt anywhere else.

He stepped up beside her. A hint of his spicy cologne mixed with his masculine scent, making the air around her delightfully intoxicating.

She breathed in deeper this time, letting her stress over the gala fade away.

He extended his arm with her wineglass. "Beautiful sight, isn't it?"

She turned to him and accepted the glass. "Yes, it is." Her gaze lingered on him. "Absolutely breathtaking."

He cleared his throat as he glanced away. "The view is the reason I took this condo." His deep voice sent a shiver of awareness down her spine. "I might have been born and bred here, but I never get tired of the views."

She continued to gaze at him. It would be so easy for her to lean back against him—to feel his firm muscled chest against her back. The thought was so enticing. The next thing she knew her body was slowly swaying toward him as if by some magnetic force.

As soon as she realized what was happening, she righted herself. What was she doing fantasizing about Silas? It wasn't like there was anything between them. There couldn't be.

Soon she'd be engaged. Her body bristled at the thought of committing herself to someone she didn't love—someone who was barely a friend at best.

Even worse, she didn't have chemistry with Matis. Certainly not like the sparks flying between her and Silas. If she was to turn around right now, would Silas wrap his arms around her and pull her close? She longed to know the answer.

But she couldn't give in to that temptation. Duty kept her facing the window. Duty to the crown meant holding herself back from giving in to her desires, but resisting this thing with Silas was taking all of her willpower.

She stepped to the side before turning to him. "This is a nice place, but I noticed you don't have a Christmas tree or any decorations. Is that something your wife or girlfriend takes care of?"

She shouldn't have asked. It was none of her business about his relationship status. And yet she couldn't squelch the burning desire to know if he'd been holding out on kissing her because of another very lucky lady.

"There's no one special in my life."

Inside her there was squeal of glee. Her heart did a flip while her stomach felt as though as swarm of butterflies had been unleashed.

On the outside, she struggled to maintain her neutral expression and nodded. She couldn't believe her ecstatic reaction to learning he was available. She'd never had that sort of reaction before. It startled her.

She rapidly searched her memory to figure out what they'd been discussing before she'd inquired about his status and then it came to her. "So, you'll be putting up the tree yourself?"

He shook his head. "I don't have a reason to decorate for myself. Besides, I don't spend that much time here."

She loved the holidays. She couldn't imagine not having a Christmas tree or the many traditions that her family indulged in each year.

"What about your mother? Does she decorate for the holidays?"

He nodded. "Definitely. Though as she's gotten older and now with my father gone, her tree has gotten smaller and smaller. Right now, she has a tabletop tree that she loves. She collects miniature ornaments for it."

"That sounds nice."

"And what about you? I assume you have a tree."

She nodded. "A great big one in the foyer. It's beautiful." There was a pang of homesickness that came over her. "It'll already be up and trimmed by the time I get home."

"I'm sorry you're missing the holidays with your family."

She restrained a sigh. So was she. "Duty comes first. There's always next year." She glanced around. "Are you ready to go?"

His dark brows drew together. "Go where?"

Her body tensed. There wasn't any time for

delays. The gala was mere days away. "Aren't we supposed to listen to the bands this evening and choose one?" When he nodded, she said, "Then let's go."

"We don't have to go anywhere."

"I don't understand."

He moved to an end table. He picked up a remote and a large wall-mounted flat-screen lit up. "They sent us their recordings. So we can relax and watch them here. You won't have to worry about anyone recognizing you and wanting selfies."

Knock-knock.

"And that would be our dinner." He moved to the door and opened it.

She glanced around the spacious room and found a table in the corner next to the window. It was all set up and there were even two tapered candlesticks. The flames flickered, sending shadows dancing across the wall, setting the stage for a cozy, romantic dinner.

If she was smart, she would turn around and walk out the door. She tried to tell herself that this was all business, but as she stared at the candles and carnations in the middle of the table, she couldn't convince herself that this dinner didn't go beyond her duty and into the realm of an intimate evening.

Instead of leaving, she took a seat at the table.

She found herself staring across the table into Silas's dark and intriguing eyes. Her heart beat faster. She longed to know more about her devastatingly handsome host.

Dinner had been full of conversation.

Silas found the Princess was more than willing to talk about her kingdom. And the more she talked, the more he wanted her to talk. He loved the sound of her sweet voice, the way her eyes lit up when she got excited and how she could draw him in with her stories of the faraway land she called home.

It was the best dinner he'd ever had and he'd barely even noticed his steak and potatoes. His full attention had been on the Princess. He could definitely get used to having dinner with her.

"Would you like dessert?" Not being sure what she would like, he'd ordered an array of desserts from triple chocolate cake to apple pie.

She set aside her napkin. "I don't think so. The stuffed flounder and rice were enough. Thank you. It was delicious." Her gaze met his. "But how did you know it's one of my favorite meals?"

"You mentioned it last night."

"I did?" She smiled. "And you remembered?"

"My job is all about paying attention to the details."

"You do your job very well."

"Are you sure about that? After all, you blamed me for this mix-up with the band."

"But we cleared that all up. Something happened and you didn't receive the email."

"So you believe me?" He told himself that her answer shouldn't matter to him but it did.

She hesitated. "I do. I'm sorry for thinking you didn't act on the email. Actually, later we found the email had gotten hung up in a draft folder."

"One mystery resolved." He reached for the remote. "Are you ready for some music?"

She reached for her glass of wine and moved to the couch. "Definitely. Let's see what we have."

"Okay." He pressed a button on the remote and the video began to play. "This is the first band. It appears both are variety bands."

"Variety bands?"

"Yes. They are cover bands that play a bunch of hit songs from eighties rock to pop."

"But do they play any dance music?"

"I don't know. Let's see." He settled on the couch near her.

The video began to play. It was a cover song he knew and they didn't do a bad job with their rendition. They sat and listened to the whole song. All the while he was acutely aware of her presence. She was so close and yet so far away.

Would it be so wrong if he wanted to shrink the distance between them? His gaze lowered to her hand as it rested on the couch near his. If he was to move his hand just a couple of inches, they would touch.

"That was pretty good, wasn't it?" Her voice drew him from his meandering thoughts.

He lifted his gaze to meet hers. "Yes, it was. Do you want to hear another song from them?"

She nodded. "Let's see if they have a variety of tunes."

And so he fast-forwarded through the video, stopping here and there to listen for a minute or two. They were good—really good. But he noticed that they didn't have a lot of variety. He had the feeling the Princess would require more versatility from the band hired for the gala.

"They were good," he said.

"Yes, they were. But we need to listen to the other band."

He switched to the next video and pressed Play. This band played some rock but they also played blues. They offered a diverse selection of music. And they were just as good as the first band, if not better.

She nodded. "Why don't you fast-forward and see if they have a different sound."

And so he did as she asked. He stopped when

they were playing a Frank Sinatra tune. *Wow!* They were definitely versatile.

As he listened to the singer croon, he got an idea. Not giving himself time to consider the right and the wrong of his action, he got to his feet. He held his hand out to her.

"What are you doing?" she asked.

"Asking you to dance."

"What? No." Color bloomed in her cheeks.

"Come on. We have to make sure they're good enough for people to dance to, don't we?"

Her brows drew together as her lips pursed. She gave him an *Are you serious?* look.

He wiggled his fingers at her. "Come on."

She hesitated a moment longer before placing her hand in his and got to her feet. He turned up the music and moved to an open space in the room. She looked up at him and smiled as he pulled her into his arms.

While the band sang about flying to the moon, he pulled the Princess close. He breathed in her gentle lavender scent. It was like a magic spell had been cast over him. He didn't want this moment to end.

She lifted her chin until their gazes met. He found her blue eyes mesmerizing. They were a blue-gray shade. He noticed how the color of her eyes would deepen depending on her mood.

His gaze lowered to her pouty lips. They provided an irresistible temptation that he was unable to avoid.

In that moment, he forgot about all the reasons that kissing her was a very bad idea. He no longer thought of how they came from totally different worlds. All he knew was that he wanted to kiss her. He wanted to know if her lips were as soft and supple as they looked.

For this second, he acted out of character by following his desire. He dipped his head and claimed her lips with his own. They were smooth and soft. And yet she didn't move.

Had he caught her entirely off guard? Hadn't she been feeling the same way as him? Had he utterly misread the entire evening? The thought filled him with dread. He was normally so good at reading people.

But then he felt her hands slowly slide up over his shoulders. Her fingers wrapped around the back of his neck and then they combed through his hair. Her nails scraped against his scalp, sending a wave of delicious sensations skittering down his arms.

Her lips moved beneath his, letting him know that he hadn't misread this moment. Perhaps it had caught her off guard just as it had him. Because desiring the Crown Princess was to desire someone who was out of his reach. Or was she?

As the kiss deepened, he knew he wanted

more—more of her kisses, more of her touches, more of Gisella. Perhaps he shouldn't write it off, especially if this kiss was any indication.

A holiday fling with the Princess would certainly brighten up his Christmas. And it wasn't like there would be any strings to worry about since Gisella had a kingdom to run far, far away. And this kiss was, oh, so good.

The vibration of the phone in his pants pocket startled him and had Gisella jumping out of his arms. Her eyes were rounded as though she was surprised by what had just taken place between them.

The rosy hue returned to her cheeks. "That… It shouldn't have happened." She moved to the couch and grabbed her red coat. "I've got to go."

"Gisella, wait. Let's talk about this."

She shook her head. "There's nothing to talk about." She stopped and stared at him. "Promise me you won't tell anyone what just happened."

He wasn't sure whether he should be amused or insulted. "I don't kiss and tell."

"Good." She moved to the door.

As her hand came to rest on the doorknob, he asked, "What band do you want for the gala?"

There was a slight hesitation. "Definitely the second one."

It was exactly what he was thinking. The music and vocals were spot-on—so much so that they'd gotten caught up in the moment and had forgotten about propriety.

Before he had a chance to utter his agreement, the door snicked shut. And he was left alone with the music still playing in the background.

For the first time in his life, he had an urge to put his interest in a woman ahead of his business. But Gisella wasn't just any woman, she was a princess.

All he had to offer her was a brief affair—it's all he ever indulged in. His business was the center of his world. And now he'd endangered their working relationship by kissing her.

It had been the most amazing kiss, but still it had been out of bounds. Now he wondered what the price would be for acting on his desires instead of following his common sense.

CHAPTER SIX

OH, MY GOODNESS!

Had that really happened?

The next day Gisella found herself replaying her time in Silas's strong arms with his lips pressed to hers. In fact, she hadn't gotten much sleep for thinking of him. And what sleep she did get was filled with dreams of Silas, and they were doing more than kissing—much more.

She was supposed to be spending the morning focused on palace work, but she had to keep rereading sentences. Her focus was severely hampered by the memory of Silas's dark eyes staring at her. She recalled the desire that had flared in them. The memory of his intense stare caused her stomach to flutter. No one had ever looked at her that boldly.

Most men tried to be sly with their passes, like they were so smart that she wouldn't catch on that they were coming on to her. Did they really think she was going to fall into bed with them?

She was born second in line for the throne. And she'd lived a very sheltered life. Her virtue had been protected for the most part—at least that's what her parents thought. What they didn't know wouldn't hurt them.

And now that she was the Crown Princess, she was expected to wait for her marriage before she had sex. It seemed so sexist that she was expected to be the epitome of virtue when no such demands had been placed upon her older brother. In fact, he was encouraged to go out and get the wild streak out of his system.

She'd never been tempted to get the "wild streak" out of her system—at least not before meeting Silas. He was changing things for her.

"Your Highness?" Eleanor, one of her two aides, looked expectantly at her.

Gisella felt a rush of panic until she realized that there was absolutely no way they could know that she was thinking of Silas. She drew in a calming breath and then turned to Eleanor. "What were you saying?"

"It's *The Duchess Tales* site. They have another story about you."

She struggled to maintain her composure. She wasn't about to let her staff see that the gossip site got to her. "I'm sure it's nothing."

"Actually, they have a photo of you entering Mr. Cabot's condo."

"What?" It wasn't until the word slipped past her lips that she bit back her next words. "I mean what will they print next? Of course I was there. He had the videos of the bands. It was all work, but I'm sure they made it out to be anything but that."

Both Eleanor and her other aide, Pearl, sent her worried looks. Gisella's heart clenched. What lies had they dredged up this time?

"Let's give the Princess some quiet time," Stephanie said.

"Thank you." She waited until they exited the suite before she reached for her phone and pulled up *The Duchess Tales*.

The website popped up on her phone. She read the headline:

GALA IN TROUBLE...

Gisella groaned. That wasn't the truth. And even if they hadn't resolved the band problem, how would the Duchess know?

She had mentioned the issue when she'd spoken to one of her staff at the palace. Was it possible someone was listening in on their phone calls?

A knock at the door caused her to inwardly groan. "Not now!"

She wanted to read the post and see if there

were any clues to lead her to the person behind the post. When the knock sounded again, she expelled a frustrated groan. She strode to the door. *This better be important.* She wasn't in the mood to be bothered.

She swung open the door. Her mouth opened to tell the person to go away, but then she saw Silas standing there. He looked utterly dashing in a dark suit with a light gray dress shirt minus the tie. The top buttons on his shirt were undone, giving her a teasing glimpse of his muscled chest.

He looked good. The man was pure eye candy and she was utterly addicted. She totally forgot what she'd been about to say.

With effort, she dragged her gaze upward to meet his. "Hi. Come on in."

"I don't mean to bother you, but you forgot this." He withdrew her green-and-red-silk scarf from his pocket. "I thought you'd want it back."

"I do." She reached out to take it from him and their fingers touched. The connection felt as though an electrical charge had arced between them. The current raced up her arm and settled in her chest, making her heart race. She refused to dwell on it. "Thank you so much." She held the scarf near her chest. "It was a gift from my late aunt so it means the world to me."

"I'm glad I could help."

She'd been so worked up since their kiss that she hadn't even noticed the scarf was missing. But she would have noticed the next time she went to put on her coat. She'd had the scarf for years and she only wore it during the holiday season.

"I'll have to pay better attention next time." The words were out of her mouth before she realized her words implied there would be a next time—alone time with Silas. And that couldn't happen. He made her wish for things that weren't hers to have.

"Your aunt must have been very special to you."

"She was. Aunt Jane was my mother's younger sister. She was the life of any social gathering. She was all smiles and loved a good joke. She was the exact opposite of my parents, which made her all the more intriguing. Truth be told, she was an enigma in my very royal, very proper family."

"But the scarf wasn't what had the worried look on your face when I arrived, was it?"

She shook her head. "There's another trouble-some post on *The Duchess Tales*."

When he sent her a puzzled look, she said, "It's a popular gossip site in Rydiania. They are known for reporting on my family. They appear to have sources well-connected with the palace."

A frown pulled at her lips. "Sometimes they report news before all of the family has been notified of the situation. It's really quite frustrating."

"I don't know why you read it. All it does is upset you."

Frustration welled up in her. "It's easy for you to say that. They aren't writing about you. But for me, well, most of Rydiania follows that gossip site. The people believe whatever they write even if they twist the truth or make up outright lies. You have no idea how much trouble they've caused for my family. My brother's wedding to the love of his life was almost called off because of the Duchess's lies."

"Why doesn't someone do something about the site?"

She sighed. "Because no one knows who's behind it."

"I see." But the look on his face said that he didn't believe it was that big of a deal. "What did the Duchess say today?"

"I don't know. I was just about to read it when you arrived." She reached for her phone and read him the title.

"That doesn't sound so bad."

"It does when my reputation as the future leader of the kingdom is resting on this international gala. This is my first time in a leadership role with the whole world watching and

Rydiania is counting on me to get this right." It wasn't until the words were out of her mouth that she realized she'd said too much.

Silas nodded. "I understand. What does the post say?"

And so she began to read aloud…

"'This most devoted royal-watcher has news about our soon-to-be Queen. It appears Princess Gisella is in New York this Christmas, hosting the Bee Global gala. This is the Princess's first big affair all on her own. If you will remember last year the King kicked off the Bee Global initiative here in Rydiania. Apparently, that wasn't good enough for the Princess and she decided to move it to New York. But now the event is in trouble. How hard can it be to organize a big holiday party? And if Princess Gisella can't arrange a party, how will she ever be able to manage a kingdom?'"

The breath caught in the back of Gisella's throat. The spiteful words sliced into her with their sharpness. The worst problem was that the post echoed her own worries.

What if the gala is a complete disaster?

"Hey." Silas moved in front of her. He placed a finger beneath her chin and lifted it until their gazes met. "Don't listen to them." He lowered his arm. "This gala is going to be a huge success. And you're going to be a great leader."

She wanted to believe him. "How can you say that? You hardly even know me."

"I know that you aren't afraid to speak up and take charge. You lead with your heart and that is something most leaders don't do."

"It's not what a strong leader would do."

"It's what a compassionate one would do."

His words resonated with her. She wanted to believe him, but dare she?

When she was second in line for the throne, she'd been so sure she could do the job, but now that circumstances had changed, she was having her doubts about her capabilities. Her father always made running the kingdom look so easy. She was learning firsthand that it wasn't as easy as it looked.

The job never ended. There were no evenings off because there was always one emergency after another. And there were no weekends off because there just weren't enough hours in the work week to handle all of the kingdom's issues. It was no wonder her father looked as though he'd aged more than his seventy-one years.

But she was up to the task, no matter what the Duchess decided to print. She wanted to make her parents and the kingdom proud of her. Most of all, she wanted to do a good job for her fellow Rydianians.

Remembering that she was reading the blog

post, she lifted her phone and scrolled down. There was a photo of her leaving Silas's building. She gasped.

Silas reached for her phone and stared at the screen. "How did they get this photo?"

"I… I don't know. Who would know I was at your place last night except my security detail?" When Silas arched a questioning brow, she said, "It wasn't one of them."

"How can you be sure?"

"Because they've worked for the palace for a long time. And all of the employees are vetted. It's not like we put out a help-wanted ad and anyone can apply. Positions are filled by connections to people who already work in the palace."

"Still, it's possible someone was in need of money and took the Duchess's offer."

She didn't want to believe it. And yet there had been one person that had been hired on for her brother's wedding and they'd ended up being a spy for the Duchess. After he was caught, they thought they'd plugged the leaks at the palace, but apparently that wasn't the case.

"What else does it say?" she asked.

He shook his head. "I don't think we need to read anymore."

"Oh, yes, we do." She took the phone out of his hand and continued to read.

This royal follower wants to know what the Princess was doing alone with Silas Cabot. Discussing business at that hour of the evening? Hardly.

Apparently, our princess is spreading her wings. What will she be up to next? Breaking with other royal protocols? Maybe she shouldn't step up to the throne. Maybe she isn't fit for the position of queen.

Gisella's stomach plummeted down to her black heels. Anger churned in her gut. How dare she?

This post was even worse than she'd thought. It was like the Duchess had it out for her personally. Was it possible she knew the Duchess? Not a chance. The Duchess was probably just some jealous know-it-all with a wild imagination.

She didn't want to keep reading, but she couldn't just ignore the piece. The people of Rydiania were going to read this and believe it was all true. How was she supposed to let them know it was nothing but lies? Well, not all lies. She had been at Silas's place the night before, but it had been for business reasons—except for that one steamy kiss.

The people of Rydiania need to be confident of their next sovereign. How can we do that when Princess Gisella isn't even here in her own kingdom?

Gisella held back a nasty comment or two. Who was this Duchess? And why did they have an ax to grind with her?

They had to be stopped. But how? She would give it some more thought. Silas's suggestion that it was someone on her staff crept into her thoughts, but it just couldn't be true.

That's all for now, royal followers. I will keep an eye on our princess and report back with updates. I know you are as concerned about this situation as I am. We can't have an inexperienced princess taking over our country, no matter who her father may be.
Until next time...

Gisella lowered the phone. Anger pumped through her veins. It was so frustrating that she didn't know who the Duchess was so they could air out these matters face-to-face.

"Don't let her get to you," Silas said in a comforting voice.

"How can I not?" She tossed her phone down on the table and paced to the other end of the room. "The Duchess is basically on the verge of calling for the people of Rydiania to overthrow the sovereign. It isn't good. And if the King hears about this—"

Buzz.

She moved to the place where she'd put her phone. She picked it up and saw that it was in fact the King. She inwardly groaned.

"Gisella, are you all right?" Silas moved to her side.

"What? Of course. Why would you ask?"

"Because all of the color drained from your face." He looked at her with concern written all over his face.

As her phone continued to ring, she knew she couldn't put off speaking to her father. "I need to get this."

"Of course."

She moved to her bedroom and closed the door. She pressed the phone to her ear. "This is Princess Gisella."

"Gisella," her father's voice rumbled through the phone. Even though he was an ocean away, it sounded like he was standing right in front of her. "What is this I hear about the gala being in trouble? Why didn't you tell me?"

"It's not true. What *The Duchess Tales* printed was exaggerated." She hated that the gossip site was causing problems within her own family. If the article could cause that sort of trouble within the palace walls, she didn't want to think of what it was causing throughout the kingdom. And there was nothing she could do about it from this great distance.

"What is the truth?"

"There was a miscommunication between my office and Silas, erm, Mr. Cabot's staff. Our band from Rydiania had to drop out of the gala due to a medical reason. For a moment, we were without a band."

"But not any longer?"

"No. Last night I met with Mr. Cabot. We reviewed some bands to fill in for the gala. And we found one that is impressive. Not only do they sound good but they also play a variety of music. I think you would approve of them."

"And this was what you were doing at his apartment?"

Her back teeth ground together. She hated how her every move was scrutinized. She didn't think her brother ever had to deal with anything like this.

"Yes. That's why I was there. Once we decided on a band, I left."

"And you couldn't have had this meeting in his offices?"

"It was late and we wanted dinner. It would have created too much fuss for us to dine in public."

"And where was your assistant during all of this?"

"She had the evening off after working late the night before."

"Gisella, you have to pay attention to appearances. This isn't good. It's time you came home."

What? Was he serious? He was ordering her home like she was some errant teenager? Anger pumped through her veins. She was upset with the Duchess for causing problems. Upset with her father for not having more faith in her. Upset at herself for forgetting her duty last night and giving in to her desires. It wouldn't happen again.

"No." Her voice was level but firm.

"What?"

"I'm not coming home. I'm not lending credence to the Duchess's words. If I do that my life as Queen will be over before my coronation. Are we any closer to catching who's behind that website?"

The King expelled a weary sigh. "I'm afraid not."

"Then I suggest we double our efforts in order to find out who is behind *The Duchess Tales*." Once again she thought about Silas's suggestion that it might be someone on her detail. She wasn't convinced, but she couldn't just outright dismiss the idea either. "Could you order another background check on everyone on my detail?"

"Your detail?" Surprise rang out in her father's voice. "You think you have a spy?"

"I don't know. But someone had to have taken that photo of me last night. And they seemed to know the details of the gala—things an outsider shouldn't have known."

"Perhaps it's someone on the PR staff."

She didn't like that thought any better. "At this point, anything is possible. I just need to be certain my staff is clear."

"I do too. I'll get some people on it. In the meantime, be careful."

"I will be. I love you, Poppi."

"I love you too."

After disconnecting the call with her father, Gisella returned to the outer room to find Silas on his phone. When he saw her, he ended his call. He looked at her with worry written all over his face.

He slid his phone into his pocket. "Is everything okay?"

She nodded. She didn't want to discuss her conversation with the King. "Everything is good." Not really but there was nothing he could do about it. She moved past him to sit down at the head of the table. "Did you get the corrections for the program to the printers?"

He nodded. "It's been taken care of."

She took a seat. "And were you able to finalize the arrangements with the television network?"

"Yes. We just have to make sure there's room for their equipment."

She opened her laptop. "Everything sounds as though it's coming along."

"It is." He moved closer. "You don't have to worry. Nothing, and no one, is going to ruin the gala."

She hoped he was right because she had so much riding on it. And the Duchess had succeeded in making the gala even a bigger deal. Now it would be a judgment of her capabilities as a queen. It wasn't fair because a production of this sort had absolutely nothing to do with running the kingdom and yet now most of Rydiania's residents would be watching the gala and judging her. She refused to let them down. She would prove to them that she was the right person to lead them into the future.

CHAPTER SEVEN

HE FELT BAD for her.

No one should have to live under such scrutiny.

Silas saw the worry lines etched around Gisella's expressive eyes. He wanted to make this better for her. He shouldn't have asked her to his penthouse, but he wasn't used to dealing with a crown princess. It was much different from an actress or an heiress as there wasn't an entire nation relying on them to make good choices.

As he watched Gisella peruse her computer, he couldn't help but think she was much like a beautiful songbird trapped in a golden bird cage. He couldn't imagine what it must be like to live the life of a royal. And even though there weren't bars on her door or windows, she must feel the restraint on her every action.

He pulled out a chair and sat down. "What are you working on?"

She glanced at him over the top of her laptop. "If you must know, I'm Christmas shopping."

"Online?"

She nodded. "I won't get home until just before Christmas. By the time I brief the King on my visit and catch up on business at the palace, there won't be time for me to shop. So, this will have to do."

"It doesn't sound very fun."

"It's shopping. It's not supposed to be fun."

"But it could be." He smiled at her as a plan started to take shape in his mind.

She shook her head. "It's not going to happen. I can't just drop into stores like everyone else. I have a security team that has to do sweeps of the places I visit. It takes a lot for me to be able to go out in public."

"Maybe it doesn't have to be so complicated."

There was a twinkle of interest in her eyes. "What do you have in mind?"

"Do you have any meetings for the rest of the day?" When she shook her head once more, he said, "Let me make a call."

She sent him a puzzled look as he stepped away and pulled out his phone. He moved toward the door to give himself a little bit of privacy just in case there was a snag with his plan. He hoped not. The Princess definitely needed some holiday cheer.

* * *

A part of her said she shouldn't do this.

And yet there was a louder part that said to go for it.

Princess Gisella sat in a chair in a private office at SC Public Relations. She'd been supplied with a pair of faded jeans, a white sweater and black ankle boots. These clothes were far from her usual proper business attire that she wore each day whether she was at the palace or elsewhere.

Silas had arranged it all. She wasn't used to letting someone call the shots aside from the King and Queen. Silas was a natural leader. He was confident, which made it easy for him to take charge.

She'd had her makeup done by a professional. The heavy makeup obscured her identity. And now she was being fitted with a blond wig. As she held up a mirror, she realized even her mother wouldn't recognize her.

The stylist held out large gold hoop earrings for her to try. She'd never worn such large earrings. Everything she wore was conservative and modest. This dress-up session was fun and freeing. She felt as though this was her last chance to have some fun before she stepped up and accepted the crown and the huge responsibility of caring for the kingdom.

"Thank you." Gisella accepted the earrings and put them on.

Knock-knock.

"Come in." She put on the earrings before turning around to find Silas standing there. "Well, what do you think?"

"Where did the Princess go?"

"Ha ha. Funny."

He stepped closer. "I'm serious. You don't look anything like yourself. There's not a chance anyone will recognize you."

"Your people did an excellent job. But I'm curious, with you being in PR, don't you want your clients to be seen and recognized?"

"Most of the time. But there are times when our clients require discretion. My job is not only to have clients be seen but also to have them seen at the appropriate times."

"I understand. So you think this will do for some Christmas shopping?"

"I certainly do. You look fantastic."

She ran her fingers through her short blond bob. "I've never been a blonde before. Let's go see if blondes really do have more fun."

As she started for the door, Silas said, "Not that way. We're going out the back."

"Oh, right. But we can't be gone long. My bodyguards will be waiting for me."

"You need to leave your phone here." He

pulled his out of his pocket and placed it on his desk. "Don't worry. It'll be safe here."

She retrieved her phone from her purse. She hesitated. She was never separated from it. It was her lifeline.

Silas's gaze met hers. "It's okay. I'll lock the room."

She placed her phone next to his. It was only for a little bit. And she knew if her absence was noticed that they'd track her through her phone. She reached for her designer bag.

"You might want to leave that too."

"You can't be serious."

He shrugged. "It's up to you, but you might not want anything that links back to your identity."

"But how am I supposed to pay for anything?"

"I'll pay for everything and you can pay me back."

She didn't like the idea of being beholden to him. And then she remembered that she had a bunch of cash in her wallet. She reached for it and withdrew the wad of twenties and hundreds. She stuffed it in her pocket.

"Let's go, Cinderella, before you turn back into a pumpkin." He sent her a teasing smile.

"Hey! I don't think I like the sound of that."

He let out a laugh. "Don't worry. You'd be a very cute pumpkin."

She gaped at him. Was he serious? "No one has ever called me a pumpkin before."

After they exited the room, he locked the door. He turned to her and smiled. He took her hand in his as he led her to the freight elevator. "Let today be full of firsts." As they made their way to the main floor, he said, "I have my car waiting for us in the alley."

His touch was warm and comforting. She knew she should pull her hand away, but she didn't want to. This was her day to do things that she didn't normally do.

And for the moment, she wasn't the Crown Princess. She was… "Hey, what's my name going to be?"

He turned a puzzled look her way. "You're Gisella."

"I don't think so. It's not that common of a name. Someone might figure things out."

"I could call you Pumpkin."

"Oh, no. Not a chance. What about Ariel?"

"Seriously? Isn't that some sort of cartoon princess?"

She shrugged. "What's wrong with the name?"

"Nothing is wrong with it. This is your day and your name. Ariel it is."

In no time at all they were in the back of a dark sedan with tinted windows. For the first time since she'd arrived in the States, she was able to take an easy breath. She leaned her head back and closed her eyes, letting all of her worries momentarily float away.

She didn't have to go shopping. She could just sit right there in the back seat next to Silas and it would be a lovely time. The more time she spent with him, the more time she wanted to spend with him.

She knew she had to be careful. She couldn't let herself fall for Silas—even though he was easy on the eyes. And he was a real-life hero. Plus, he was going out of his way for her. It was a lot to resist.

"Why are you doing all of this?" she asked.

"What? Taking you shopping?"

"And the makeover. I know you have work to do. Why are you taking time out of your day to spend it with me?"

He reached for her hand, lacing his long fingers with hers. "Do you really have to ask?"

Her mind immediately went back to the kiss they'd shared not even twenty-four hours ago. Her gaze met his. It would be so easy to lean over and press her lips to his. She wanted to do that more than she wanted anything else in that moment.

And yet she resisted the temptation. "We can't have a repeat of last night. You understand that, don't you?"

"Well, Ariel, I don't remember seeing you last night." He leaned over and whispered, "I spent my evening with a beautiful princess."

His breath fanned over her ear, sending a shiver of desire cascading over her skin. He was flirting with her and she had absolutely no interest in stopping him.

She smiled and shook her head. "Don't let yourself get caught up in this fantasy you've created."

"Why? It's fun. Where do you want to go first?"

"A toy store. I want to get a gift for my little nephew."

"How old is he?"

"Well, he hasn't been born yet. My youngest sister is pregnant and living in the South of France with her husband. I've never seen her happier. And they're going to be at the palace for Christmas so I want to have something special for the baby."

His eyes widened. "So you're starting early."

"Starting what early?"

"Campaigning to be his favorite aunt."

The thought made her smile. "Yes, I am."

Being around Silas helped her to see the world in a different way—a good way. It wasn't all about public perceptions. There was room—not much, but a little room—for her to enjoy herself. It was something she hadn't done since her brother stepped out of line for the throne.

Was it a bit selfish? Yes, it was. Did she feel guilty? Not really. She had dedicated her life to public service. If this trip to New York was her only chance to let loose and have a good time—she could live with it. And the memories would keep her company when the going got tough—and it would. She'd watched her parents and contrary to popular thought their lives were not all royal balls and state dinners. There were tough times in between.

She looked out the window as the snow began to fall in big, lazy flakes. In the store windows were Christmas lights and holiday displays. Then she turned to Silas and found him staring back at her. With his fingers still laced with hers, his thumb stroked the back of her hand, sending her heart racing.

CHAPTER EIGHT

HER FACE LIT UP.

A smile lifted the corners of her rosy lips.

Silas was captivated by Gisella, erm… Ariel as she had fun shopping. They made their way up and down every aisle of the toy store. By the way she acted he'd swear she'd never been in a toy store. Was that possible?

He wouldn't know the answer. He honestly didn't know much about the life of a royal. But he loved her animation as she found a new toy to marvel over.

They started with no basket and no cart. Then they had too many toys and stuffed animals to hold so he grabbed a basket. It wasn't long until he'd had to get a cart. Now he was worried there might not be enough room in the car for everything.

He stepped up beside her as she tried to decide between a plush pink flamingo security blanket and a llama one. "Are you sure your nephew needs all of this stuff?"

Gisella placed both blankets in the cart before turning to him. "It's not all for my nephew."

"Then who is the other stuff for?"

"Mary and Susie. With them losing their home, it's going to be a rough Christmas for them. I just thought some of this might cheer them up."

He was surprised by how thoughtful she could be. When she'd had them stop by the hospital after they'd first met, he'd wondered if it was some sort of photo op. It wasn't until they were there and she was going around doing selfies with the other sick children and their families that he realized she was a caring person.

He supposed he'd worked in this business for too long. He was used to being around people who were consumed with themselves and what was good for their image.

When he looked at Gisella, he saw the most beautiful woman in the world. Her beauty started with her very generous and caring heart and worked its way outward. He longed to remove her disguise to reveal her mesmerizing blue eyes that were now hidden behind brown contacts. Her eyelashes were accentuated with fake ones. And her eyes were highlighted with heavy eye makeup. She definitely didn't look like herself. But even with the disguise she was a knockout.

It was all he could do not to reach out and

pull her into his arms. But he noticed that no one had given her a second glance. Her disguise was holding up.

And so when she turned to him with a purple teddy bear in her hands and a pouty look on her face, he was drawn to her. It was a magnetic force that he was unable to fight—not that he wanted to be deterred. Her lush lips couldn't be disguised and they were so very tempting.

He stepped up to her and stared deep into her eyes. His heart pounded and for the first time he was at a loss for words. Instead of speaking, he dipped his head and claimed her lips.

Her lips were soft and warm. She kissed him back, making his heart pound against his ribs. He longed to reach out and draw her to him, but he resisted the urge because they were in public. He didn't trust himself to deepen their kiss for fear that things would spiral out of control.

Someone behind him cleared their throat. "Excuse me."

Gisella practically jumped away from him. As he moved their cart off to the side, he noticed the rosy hue in Gisella's cheeks. He didn't think she could look any more adorable but he was wrong.

After they checked out, he helped the driver load the gifts into the trunk and joined Gisella in the back seat. With the divider up, they were afforded some privacy. He should probably apologize for his spontaneous kiss, but he didn't want to apologize because he didn't want to take it back. Still, it was the right thing to do.

He turned to her. "Gisella…"

Before he could say another word, she leaned toward him. And then her lips pressed to his. He reached out to her. His fingers caressed her check as he deepened the kiss. He'd never wanted anyone as much as he wanted her.

He pulled back ever so slightly. His breathing was heavy. His heart was racing. "Let's go back to my place."

She hesitated. "I can't."

"Sure you can. No one will recognize you."

"But my staff will miss me. As it is, I've already been gone too long."

There had to be a way for them to be together without her staff. He couldn't believe at his age he was sneaking around. He thought his days of that were over when he was a teenager. And yet even that thought couldn't deter him.

"What about tonight?" he asked.

"Tonight?"

He nodded. "Can't you sneak out of your suite? Surely your bodyguards don't camp out in front of your door."

"No. They're at the end of the hall. We have the whole wing reserved for security reasons."

"So you could put on your disguise and take the steps."

She looked at him. "You're serious, aren't you?"

"Of course I am." Suddenly he worried he was the only one who was serious about taking this thing between them to the next level. "Unless you're not interested."

"I don't know. I've never ditched my detail before and now you're asking me to do it twice in one day."

"All you have to do is exit the hotel and my car will be waiting for you. We'll take off and have you back before anyone even notices you're gone."

She raised her hand. Her fingertip trailed down his jaw and ran temptingly over his lips. He caught her fingertip between his teeth and then he licked it. He saw her eyes widen with surprise.

He released her finger. "Am I convincing you?"

"Maybe… I might need a little more convincing."

He reached out to her and drew her close. With his lips a fraction of an inch from hers, he asked, "Is this what you had in mind?"

And then he pressed his lips to hers. The kiss immediately grew hot and steamy. He should be careful of smudging her disguise, but his desire was running high and his common sense was rapidly diminishing.

He didn't want to wait until that night to see her again. It would be the sweetest torture he'd ever experienced. But having time alone with Gisella would be worth it.

She couldn't sit still.

Every time Gisella sat down at her computer to do some work, she would become distracted with thoughts of Silas. She'd decided that he was quite dangerous. He liked to take chances and that wasn't like her. She was the rule follower—the proper princess.

And now he had her donning disguises and running off with him to have fun. It was so unlike her. And yet when she thought of him, her heart raced and her stomach fluttered.

If she was smart, she'd have turned him down. She wouldn't be waiting for the coast to be clear. She wouldn't have already thought up the excuses that would give her a quiet evening where no one would notice her absence.

What was wrong with her? Why was she acting like some school-age girl with the biggest crush on the most handsome boy in the school?

The truth of the matter was that she'd never been in love before. She didn't know if it was that she hadn't let herself get close enough to a guy to have feelings for him or if it was the fact that she knew falling in love with someone was pointless because her parents had her future planned out. And there was absolutely no room in those plans for love.

As a royal, her life revolved around duty to the crown. She had to do what was best for the family, for the king and for the kingdom. It wasn't that she never got to have fun. It was that she never had the freedom.

Buzz.

She reached for her phone. She wasn't sure who it would be. She'd told her assistant and aides they could have the evening off to go to the theater.

When she checked the caller ID and saw that it was her youngest sister, Cecelia, she immediately pressed the phone to her ear. "Cecelia, is everything okay?"

"Well, that's certainly some greeting. And yes, everything is fine with me and your nephew. Although he is an active little guy. That is when he's not sitting on my bladder."

Gisella breathed a sigh of relief. "That's good to hear. I can't wait to hold him."

"It won't be much longer."

"So what has you calling?"

"I just wanted to check in. I'm not disturbing you, am I?"

"No, not at all."

Cecelia was not only the youngest in the family but the most adventurous. She lived her life in equal portions, part in duty to the crown and the other part with a duty to her own happiness. It drove their parents crazy. Especially Cecelia's latest episode when she took off to the South of France and ended up meeting her husband.

And that's why Cecelia was the perfect person for this conversation. Her sister was in a position to understand Gisella's conflicting emotions—emotions she'd never had before.

"Is everything all right?" Cecelia asked.

"Of course." *Liar.* "Why are you asking?"

"Because you don't quite sound like yourself."

This was her moment to say something. She just didn't know if she wanted her sister to talk her into this crazy scheme or to talk her out of it.

"Can I confide in you?"

"Of course."

"But it has to stay just between the two of us. You can't tell your husband and certainly no one in the family."

"Now you have me worried. Of course you can trust me."

"I mean it. You have to swear you won't mention what I'm going to tell you to anyone."

"Yes, I swear. Now what's going on?"

And so she told Cecelia about her first meeting with Silas and how she'd totally misjudged him. She mentioned how he was a real-life hero and she even told her about sneaking out to go Christmas shopping.

"Wow." There was a pause as though Cecelia was trying to process all of this information. "But what about Matis? Aren't you two supposed to marry someday?"

Gisella sighed. "Yes."

"But you don't want to marry him, do you?"

For so long, Gisella had been holding in all of her feelings—telling herself they didn't matter—telling herself the only thing that mattered was her duty to the crown. But she was starting to see that there was more to life than just the crown. There was so much she was missing out on by not being honest with herself and others.

"No, I don't. It's not that Matis isn't nice enough. I… I just can't imagine spending the rest of my life with him. I don't even want to kiss him."

"You haven't kissed him yet?"

"No." She wasn't even tempted. "And to be honest, I don't think he's any more into me than I am into him."

"I see. But you like kissing Silas?"

She *loved* kissing Silas. Two kisses just weren't enough. "Yes."

"And you feel safe with him?"

"As safe as I've ever felt in my life."

"Then I say you should go this evening and let yourself enjoy the time you have with him. You've never let yourself have the freedom to find what truly makes you happy. I think this is the perfect time to do it."

"But I worry about *The Duchess Tales*. I still don't know who's behind it. Silas thinks it might be someone on my staff."

"You said your disguise was so good that you went shopping in New York City and no one spotted you, right?"

"Yes. I even checked *The Duchess Tales* when I got back to my suite to see if there were any updates but there was nothing." She'd been checking the site all evening just to be certain there wasn't some sort of delay with the post, but there was still nothing.

"It's totally up to you, but I've never seen you so into a guy before. I think you should meet him and enjoy yourself. When tomorrow comes you can return to being the proper crown princess and no one will be the wiser."

They talked for a few more minutes. Afterward, Gisella verified that her staff was away for the evening and wouldn't be back until late. She told her security detail that she had a headache and was turning in early for the night. She instructed them that she wasn't to be disturbed.

And then Gisella put their plan in motion.

The makeup artist had shown her how to put on the costume makeup. Her application wasn't as good, but it would pass. And then she put on the blond wig. She couldn't deny it was fun to dress up as someone else. There was definitely a sense of liberation in the act.

Simon said he'd arranged for someone to come to her floor and distract her security team just long enough for her to slip down the corridor to the steps. And he would be waiting for her outside in his chauffeured sedan.

She was nervous and excited all at the same time. She'd never done anything like this and now she was doing it twice in one day. With her hair and makeup complete, all she had to do was wait for Silas's signal.

CHAPTER NINE

His deal was in trouble.

Silas had worked hard to build his flourishing company that now had a handful of offices up and down the East Coast. And now was his chance to expand to the West Coast. He was so close, but then he let himself become distracted with the gorgeous Princess.

He shouldn't have played hooky all afternoon. If he had been at his office like he was supposed to be, he would have received the call that the West Coast company he hoped to merge with had read the headlines that the gala was in trouble.

When he'd returned their call, he'd tried to reassure them via a videoconference call that everything was on track with the gala, but they countered with rumors that had been started by *The Duchess Tales* and had been picked up by some of the American news outlets.

They informed him that they were looking at

another company to merge with. The news was like a gut punch. There was no way he was losing out to another company.

In desperation to stay in the competition, he invited them to the gala. When they didn't immediately bite, he said he would introduce them to the Princess as he was going to be her escort. He hoped Gisella would go along with his plan. He didn't see it would be a problem as she had spent the day with him and the evening held such promise.

He hated that he'd worked this hard to be at the top of his game and now he felt as though he were auditioning for this merger. It grated on his nerves. But he also realized that once the merger was complete, his company would be bigger than ever. It would be the number one PR firm from coast to coast.

After he completed the tense conversation, he set to work on his plans for the evening. He intended to make this evening a time Gisella wouldn't forget. With the aid of his assistant, they created a little bit of magic.

And now he sat in the car outside Gisella's hotel, hoping her disguise held up and she was able to slip away unnoticed. He wanted to go inside to get her, but he knew if any of her staff saw him it would make it more difficult for her.

His knee bounced up and down as he stared

out the car window. He peered into the night searching for a petite blonde.

As the minutes went by, he started to worry that she'd been spotted by her team. Maybe this hadn't been the smartest idea. Maybe he shouldn't have pushed things with her.

And then he remembered the way she'd kissed him back. There had been passion in her touch. In her eyes he'd seen a desire to let loose and have some fun. Something told him that she rarely, if ever, relaxed and enjoyed herself. He wanted tonight to be special for her.

But she still wasn't coming. Worry knotted his gut. He didn't want to get her in trouble. Wait. Could a princess get in trouble? He supposed so since she reported to the King and Queen.

He reached for his phone to message her. As his fingers moved over the screen, he paused and glanced up. There was Gisella exiting the hotel. She paused outside the door. Her head turned left and then right. Her disguise was perfectly in place and no one seemed to realize that she was in fact a princess.

He forced himself not to get out and hold the door for her. His knee bounced up and down even faster. They were *so* close to pulling this off.

When she was at last in the car next to him, he took his first easy breath. "You look amazing."

"Thank you." It was too dark in the car to know for sure, but in his mind, he envisioned her cheeks taking on a rosy hue.

"So you got away undetected?"

"I did."

She exhaled a sigh and leaned back against the seat. He reached out and took her hand in his. She turned to look at him and smiled. It caused a funny feeling in his chest. He chose not to examine it too closely.

In no time they were back at his penthouse. He opened the door for her and followed her inside. She stopped a few steps inside his place.

While he took off his coat, she stood still staring at the ten-foot spruce tree in front of the window. It was trimmed with white twinkling lights.

"I don't understand," she said. "There wasn't a Christmas tree here yesterday."

"I know. I had some time on my hands today. And I was hoping you would help me decorate it." He gestured toward the boxes of ornaments on the dining table.

She turned to him. "But you don't do Christmas decorations."

"I don't but you do. And I know how much you're missing your family at this time of the year and I thought you might like this."

Her face lit up. "You did all of this for me?"

"I did."

He'd never made a grand gesture like this for any other woman. He'd never been inspired to go out of his way for anyone but Gisella. And just seeing the way her face lit up, he knew it was well worth his effort.

He used a remote and lit up a strand of garland draped over the mantle. And then he lit the fireplace. He moved to the coffee table and lit a trio of candles. In the background, "White Christmas" began to play.

He turned to her and helped her off with her coat. He draped it over the couch and then he turned to her. "Did you eat yet?"

"I'm afraid I did. I hope you're not upset."

"Not at all. It just means we can move on to this." He held his hand out to her. "May I have this dance?"

"Yes, you may." She placed her hand in his, and he drew her near.

She felt so good pressed up against him. He inhaled her lavender scent. His worries and stress of the day faded away. He let himself live in the moment. Her head came to rest on his shoulder. He could get used to this—very used to it. It was as though she belonged in his arms.

When the song ended, she pulled back. "Thank you for today. I can't tell you how much I've enjoyed it."

"Me too." He stared deeply into her eyes. He noticed that tonight she hadn't put in the brown contacts. Instead, he found himself staring into her vibrant cornflower blue eyes and feeling himself drowning in their intensity.

In that moment, he wanted to pull her back into his arms and kiss her, but he resisted the urge. He didn't want her to think he'd invited her to his place just for that. He had the evening planned and maybe they'd circle back around to the kissing.

"Would you like to help me decorate the tree?" He moved to the table.

"Are you serious?"

"Of course. Why wouldn't I be?"

"I don't know. It's your tree."

"And I thought we could decorate it together."

"Okay." She moved to his side and started to check out the ornaments. "But first I need to go do something. Can you point me in the direction of the bathroom?"

A few minutes later Gisella returned minus her wig and heavy makeup. Even without any makeup on, she was absolutely stunning.

"Are you going to put all of the makeup back on before you leave?" he asked.

She shook her head. "No. I don't like sneaking around. If I'm spotted returning, I'll just deal with it."

He smiled. He didn't like the sneaking around either. "Sounds like a plan. And if you need a backup, let me know."

"Thanks. But I'll be fine."

After they put some ornaments on the tree, he asked, "Are you enjoying spending the holidays in the city?"

"I am. Thanks to you." She opened a box of silver ball ornaments.

"Anything you want to do that you haven't done yet?"

Her eyes momentarily widened with surprise. "I'm good."

"Come on. There has to be something special you want to do." When she looked at him there was this look in her eyes as though she'd thought of something, prompting him to say, "What is it?"

She shook her head. "It's nothing."

"It's definitely something. Out with it."

"Has anyone ever told you that you're persistent?"

A smile pulled at the corners of his lips. "Perhaps. Now do tell."

"Okay. I wanted to see the Rockettes while I'm here, but I already checked and their show is sold out."

"That's too bad. Are you sure?"

She nodded as she searched for the ornament hooks.

And so, for the next hour, they hung ornaments on the tree. He put hooks on the ornaments and she placed them on the tree. He wasn't big on Christmas but the tree didn't look so bad.

He stepped back to take in the full sight. "Looks nice."

Gisella stood beside him. "It's missing something."

"It is?" He didn't see how that was possible when it looked like there were hundreds of ornaments all over it.

"Yes." She lightly elbowed him. "It needs the angel on top."

She moved to the table and picked up the box with the angel in it—the angel his assistant insisted that he buy. Apparently, Gladys was right. He owed her an extra-big Christmas bonus.

"Can you give me a hand with the ladder?" She adjusted the angel's gown.

"Sure. Where do you want it?"

She pointed to a spot next to the tree. And then she climbed it while he steadied it for her. She placed the angel at the top and plugged it in so the lights in the angel's hands lit up.

"Does it look right?" she asked.

He took a step to the side and stared up at the tree. "It looks perfect."

She started down the ladder. She was wearing high heels. The second step from the bottom, her foot slipped. Silas automatically reached out, catching her in his arms.

She wrapped her arms around his neck. "Sorry about that."

"I'm not. Now I have you right where I want you." He leaned his head forward and placed a kiss on her lips.

He didn't know that a kiss could be so sweet. He was totally addicted to her. He didn't think he'd ever get enough.

With the greatest of regret, he lowered her feet to the floor. "We have more to do."

"We do? But the tree is done."

"Come this way." He took her hand and led her to the kitchen.

"What are we going to do here?"

"We're going to bake Christmas cookies."

She gaped at him before she started to laugh. "Are you serious?"

"Of course I am. What's Christmas without cookies?"

"Do you know how to bake?"

He shook his head. "I don't have a clue."

"Neither do I. So how do you propose we go about this?"

"I thought that might be the case." He moved to the fridge and withdrew a plastic wrapped tube of cookie dough. "That's why I got ready-to-bake cookies. Think you can turn the oven on while I find the baking sheets?"

Baking cookies was not what he wanted to do right now. But this was a real-life princess and he wanted to take things slow. He wasn't even sure where they were headed, though he did have some very definite thoughts on the subject.

Tree-trimming.

And cookie-baking.

Two days later, she still couldn't get it out of her mind. It had been a wonderful evening and not the one Gisella had been expecting. She'd thought it would be a more intimate evening.

She reflected on how Silas acted when he was decorating the cookies. He'd been so focused. Twin lines had formed between his brows as he worked. And then he'd paused to watch her and his eyes had filled with amusement as she'd made a mess of things.

When they'd both reached for the frosting at the same time, their fingers had touched. The thrill of the connection had raced up her arm and settled in her chest. She recalled how their gazes had met and held. Time had seemed to suspend. Her heart had pitter-pattered with excitement and happiness. No one had ever made her feel so much at one time.

She couldn't help but wonder if she was giving up these types of moments in order to become the queen. Would she never know again the thrill of a casual touch or the pulsing desire to feel another's lips pressed to hers?

Refusing to contemplate the answer to the question, she pushed aside the thought. It wasn't easy. Silas had opened her eyes to what she'd be missing by letting her duty dictate her life. And now she didn't know how she'd ever be content with a loveless marriage.

She'd enjoyed talking with Silas and getting to know him better. He'd told her about his childhood Christmases and how his mother used to bake the entire week leading up until Christmas. And then on Christmas Eve, he and his mother would deliver cookie trays to the neighbors.

It sounded like a nice memory. She had nothing like it to compare. Her mother was lucky if she knew where the kitchen was and the Queen knew nothing about baking. But her mother had a lot of other skills that helped people on a daily basis.

Gisella had noticed how Silas never mentioned his father. She wondered about that but she didn't inquire. She had the feeling if he'd wanted to talk about his father, he would have brought him into the conversation.

The last couple of days, they'd gone over the

playlist for the band. It was a mix of holiday music and contemporary tunes. They'd also finalized the seating chart. It was no easy feat.

The invitation list comprised politicians, celebrities, media people and scientists. It wasn't easy to get the right mix of people at each table that would invite friendly conversation. And then there was research on social media to see which personality wasn't getting along with another personality. The last thing she wanted was for the gala to make headlines for all of the wrong reasons.

After their ordered-in lunch, Silas approached her. "How would you feel about having some fun this evening?"

"I… I don't know." She glanced around at the work on the conference table. "There's still things to be done before the gala."

"I think we're in a good enough place for you to take the evening off."

"Shh…" She glanced around, making sure no one had overheard them. Luckily everyone was on the other side of the room talking among themselves. Softly she said, "I think I need to keep working on these arrangements."

"Even if I told you that I got us tickets to Radio City Music Hall to see the Rockettes Christmas special?"

Her mouth gaped. "You did?"

He smiled and nodded. "You said you wanted to go."

"But the tickets are sold out."

"Oh, I know a person that knows a person."

She whispered, "I want to hug you right now but I can't."

"Does that mean you'll go with me?"

She hesitated. "I don't know. I can't afford more bad press. And I still don't know who's spying on me."

"But would going to the theater really be bad press? Think about it. Do the people of Rydiania want a queen who's serious all of the time? Or do they want someone who knows how to smile and is willing to spend time like normal people? Someone that in some small way they can identify with."

"I…" She pressed her lips together. "I hadn't thought of it that way."

Her parents adhered to the royals having an air of mystery about them. They didn't share much with the public about their personal lives. In fact, they made a point of sharing as little as possible. Did she want to start her reign in the same manner?

Would *The Duchess Tales* be such a big deal if her family were to share more about themselves? With the *huge* popularity of that gossip site, it was obvious that the people of Rydiania were longing for a greater connection to the royal family. Perhaps the time had come for a little more transparency with the palace. It was definitely a subject she intended to give a lot more thought.

"What do you say? Shall we go to the theater? Or should I give away the tickets?" There was a hopeful glint in his dark eyes.

"I'd love to go with you."

"Will you be able to sneak away again?"

She shook her head. "I'm done with the disguises. This time I'm going as myself."

His brows lifted. "Are you sure you want to do that?"

"I'm positive. Sneaking around is not my thing. It never was and after the other day, it only confirmed that I don't like doing it."

"And will your family have a problem with it?"

"I wouldn't think so, but even if they do, I'm a grown woman and capable of making up my own mind. After all, soon I'll be responsible for an entire kingdom. I think I can decide on whether to go to the theater on my own."

A smile came over his face and smoothed his worry lines. "Then it's a date."

She liked the sound of that. "It is."

Now she had to tell her staff, although she would leave the part out about it being a date.

She'd merely explain that Siłas was being polite and showing her around the city. It sounded innocent enough in her mind.

CHAPTER TEN

The evening was amazing.

Her date was entertaining.

And the night wasn't over yet.

Gisella felt as though her feet were touching the clouds as Silas escorted her around the city. There were paparazzi and photos—lots of photos. But Silas put her at ease and had her laughing throughout their meal as he told her tales of his childhood and the escapades he got into.

The more time she spent with him, the more she got to know him. He was like an onion where she had to keep peeling back the layers. He continued to intrigue her.

The Rockettes didn't disappoint. They were even more impressive than Gisella had ever imagined, but not as great as her date. She reached out, placing her hand over his as they sat in the back of his sedan.

When he turned to her, she said, "Thank you. It's been an evening I'll never forget."

"Me either." He squeezed her hand.

Her heart pitter-pattered. She'd never felt this way with anyone. She knew she couldn't get in too deeply because all too soon, royal protocols would dictate that she marry someone else—someone she didn't love.

As soon as the thought came to her, she banished it to the back of her mind. She wasn't going to let anything ruin this magical evening. She wondered if this was how both of her sisters felt when they'd been on a date with their now husbands. Not that she was thinking of Silas as husband material—at least not for her.

"Where are we going?" She stared out the window at the holiday lights at the various businesses.

"I have one more surprise for you."

She glanced back at him. "Another surprise?"

He nodded. "And don't ask where because I'm not telling you."

"Not even if I beg?"

"Not even then."

She sighed as she settled back against the seat. It was cold out but it wasn't snowing. Even without the fluffy white stuff, the city looked like it was ready for Santa to make a visit.

There was a vibrancy to the city that she hadn't felt back in Rydiania. It was hard to explain but she liked it. Maybe not enough to live in New York City, but she certainly liked to visit it.

And then the car slowed and stopped. Her door was opened and she stepped out on the sidewalk in front of the Empire State Building. She craned her neck, looking up at the stately building.

She turned to Silas. "What are we doing here?"

His brows drew together, forming twin lines. "Have you already been here?"

She shook her head. "No. Never."

His brow smoothed. "Good." He presented his arm to her. "Shall we?"

She placed her hand in the crook of his arm. "We shall."

They made their way inside. She let Silas guide her to some of the exhibits. He told her they had a bit of time to waste until their ticketed time to visit the observation deck. She enjoyed reading about the history of the building. And she got a laugh out of the King Kong exhibit.

People would stop and stare at them, but thankfully they didn't bother them for selfies or autographs. She wondered if their evening would make it into *The Duchess Tales*. As soon as the thought crossed her mind, she pushed it away. She wasn't going to let the Duchess ruin this evening.

At last, it was their time to visit the observation deck. It was breezy up there but with Silas by her side, she didn't notice the cold so much. They moved to an open spot on the observation deck. She peered out at the lights of the city. Silas led her over to one of the viewfinders, where he dropped some coins in the machine and gestured for her to step up. He didn't have to ask her twice.

She moved to the viewfinder and looked out at the city. It was awe-inspiring. She'd never experienced anything quite like it. This whole evening had been marvelous and it was all thanks to Silas.

She stepped back. "You should have a look. It's an amazing view."

"I already have the most beautiful view right in front of me."

"Shh…" She glanced around to make sure no one had overheard him. Thankfully no one seemed to notice. "But thank you. Now go ahead and look through that… What do you call it?"

"A viewfinder." He placed some more coins in the machine and then peered through it. When he stepped back, he whispered, "It was a great view, but I still prefer the one in front of me."

Heat warmed her cheeks. She whispered back, "Mine is pretty great too."

She had the feeling he was tempted to kiss her because she felt the same way, but this wasn't the place for anything like that. It was way too public.

As a way to distract them both from temptation, she reached for her phone. "Let's take a selfie."

"Okay. Where do you want me?"

They turned their backs to the city. She held out the phone. No matter how far out she stretched her arm, they both weren't fully in the frame.

"Get closer," she said. He moved but it still wasn't enough. "A little closer."

He leaned his head against hers.

"Perfect." She snapped the picture.

She knew she would stare at this picture long after she left New York. This was the most wonderful day of her life. The enormity of the thought wasn't missed by her. She just chose not to dwell on it. Instead, she returned her focus to the sexy man beside her.

This was a special night.

He couldn't remember the last time he'd relaxed and enjoyed himself so much.

Silas didn't think he'd ever had a more enjoyable evening. There was something so special about Gisella. And it had absolutely nothing to do with her being a princess.

He didn't want this evening to end. He struggled to figure out a way to extend it. He knew with the gala just days away that soon she would be gone. And he wanted to spend as much time with her as possible.

He turned to her. "Come on. I have another surprise for you."

"Another? You're spoiling me."

"And loving every minute of it."

He took her hand in his and led her to a special elevator. He might have bribed the attendant to let them go to the top by themselves. He just needed a moment of this special evening to be all about themselves without any curious onlookers.

Once they stepped onto the elevator and the door slid shut, he turned to her. "Are you really enjoying yourself?"

"Yes, Silas. I really am. Thank you." As the elevator began to move, she said, "Wait. No one is riding with us."

"Not this time. I thought a little alone time was in order."

"But we're not going down."

"No," he said. "We're going up."

"I didn't know you could go any higher."

"Just wait and see."

When the elevator reached the 102nd floor, the glass elevator gave a jaw-dropping view of the city in all directions. He'd never been up this high and he was glad he got to experience this moment with Gisella.

She gasped. "We're on top of the world."

The elevator had floor-to-ceiling windows the whole way around it. He actually felt as though he was on top of the world and what made it even more special was having the most beautiful woman next to him.

"Look." She pointed. "You can see the Statue of Liberty."

"I take it you approve of your surprise?"

"I do. I really do." She turned to him and lifted up on her tiptoes so she could press her lips to his.

He returned her kiss. In the darkness of the evening, they wrapped their arms around each other. Nothing in his life had ever felt so right as it did at this particular moment.

For years, he'd been focused on his business—on building it to be bigger and better. He'd always thought when he grew successful enough that he would feel fulfilled. It had never happened—until now. Gisella filled in the cracks in his heart and made him feel whole.

When she pulled back enough to stare into his eyes, he cradled her face between his hands. Her cheeks were growing cold. Just then big lazy snowflakes drifted down around the elevator.

"I hope you enjoyed the evening," he said.

"I did. I've never had such a wonderful evening. I don't want it to end."

He stared deep into her eyes. "Do you really mean that?"

She nodded. "I do. But it has to."

He checked the time. "It isn't that late. Would you like to come back to my place?" When the worry shone in her eyes, he said, "We can go into the private parking garage and ride up to my place in an express elevator. The press won't see you."

"I don't know."

He knew he had to sweeten the offer without putting too much pressure on her. "We could sip some hot chocolate next to the Christmas tree."

With a blink of her eyes, the worry disappeared. "I'd like that."

"I would too." He pulled her close and pressed his lips to her.

The spectacular view was quickly forgotten. Soon they were back on the ground in his sedan, speeding back to his penthouse. Without anyone to notice, the car pulled into the garage. Other than her bodyguards, no one saw them step into his private elevator and head for his penthouse.

He didn't know what to expect for the remainder of the evening. He had his hopes. But did she want the same thing? His gaze momentarily dipped to her glossy lips. Would their expectations for the evening align?

Just as he promised, he made them some gourmet hot chocolate that he'd purchased with Gisella in mind. With the tree lights lit and the fireplace going, they settled on the couch. This was really cozy—cozier than he'd ever been in the penthouse.

When he glanced at her, he noticed her cheeks and nose were still tinged with pink from the cold. "Let me grab you a blanket."

"It's not necessary."

"But you're cold. I'll be right back." He moved swiftly to his linen closet and pulled out one of the throw blankets his mother insisted on buying him for Christmas each year. He'd be willing to wager when his mother purchased the blanket that she'd never imagined that one day it would be keeping a princess warm. A smile lifted the corner of his lips.

When he returned to the living room, he found Gisella gazing into the fireplace. He wondered what she was thinking about. He hoped it wasn't anything stressful.

He sat down next to her. "A penny for your thoughts."

She turned to him with a little smile. "Is that all my thoughts are worth to you?"

"I don't know. Tell me what they are and then I'll reevaluate."

"I was thinking I'm so comfortable with the fire, the tree and you that I could just stay here all night."

He definitely liked the direction of her thoughts. "Sounds good to me." He slipped his arm over her shoulder and drew her to his side. Her head landed on his shoulder. "Why don't you stay?"

"Because I can't."

"I don't see anyone coming to drag you away."

"Trust me, it will cause a lot of problems— problems I just can't have in my life right now."

He didn't like being labeled a problem. He'd much rather be called a wonderful date or better yet a terrific lover. Maybe she needed a little more convincing.

He placed a kiss atop her head. She pulled away. His hopes sank.

He sighed. "I'm sorry."

"It's not you. It's me."

"Really? Because I was thinking that right up until now, we were having a really good time together."

"We were…um, we are." She shifted on the couch so she could look at him. "It's just that things like this don't normally happen for me because I'm a princess. And now that I'm the Crown Princess, everything has changed."

"What does that mean?"

Her gaze lowered and she hesitated. "It means when I get serious about someone they have to be of royal descent."

"And what if they aren't?" The breath hitched in his throat as he awaited her answer.

"It won't happen. I won't let it." There was a resolute tone in her voice.

Her insistence touched on a nerve that had him pushing the subject. "But what if it does?"

Her eyes momentarily widened at his insistence. After a strained moment, she said, "Being the Crown Princess means I have to follow certain royal protocols. By the kingdom's charter, I can't marry them."

In other words, he wasn't good enough for her. The words stabbed at him. Unwanted memories surfaced in his mind. For so many years, he'd heard his father constantly telling him that he wasn't good enough.

Even from the grave his father had made sure Silas knew what he thought of him. He'd left his money to Silas's mother, as he should have, but when it came to his precious business, he'd left it to the man who'd worked his way up in the business to become the vice president.

Silas had no place in his father's will. He didn't even rank so much as a mention. It was as though he didn't even exist as far as his father was concerned. Not that it was a surprise, but it just drove home the loathing his father had for him.

When he was young, he'd have done anything to please his father—to prove that he was worthy of a place in his father's life. Just like now, he wanted to prove to Gisella that he could go shoulder to shoulder with those guys with royal blood. But he knew no matter what he said or did that he couldn't come out on top. He was once again not good enough.

The acknowledgment stung. He told himself it wasn't like he wanted anything serious with her. This was just a fling—possibly.

He cleared his throat. "It's a good thing this thing between us is just casual. You know…no strings attached."

She sent him a tentative smile. "I agree."

He let out a deep breath. "How did we get onto the subject of marriage?" He sent her a playful smile. It seemed as though their expectations were aligning. "We could just enjoy ourselves. No harm. No foul."

When she stared into his eyes, he could see the struggle waging within her. He wanted to make this all right for her, but he wasn't going to pressure her. Whatever happened from here was totally up to her and he would be fine with it—at least that's what he wanted to convince himself of.

But he'd never desired someone as much as he did her. He knew that soon she'd be gone and something told him that he would miss her presence in his life. Not that he was getting attached or anything. Because he didn't let himself need people. The only person he could rely on was himself.

Still, his life seemed so much brighter with Gisella in it. In fact, for the first time since he was a kid, it felt like a merry Christmas. Too bad she wouldn't be here for the big day.

She checked the time. It was almost eleven o'clock. "Don't forget I turn into a pumpkin at midnight."

"You'd be such a cute pumpkin."

She frowned at him. "I don't think that's a compliment."

"I don't know. Why don't you stay past midnight and we'll find out?"

"I think you're wasting time." Her eyes flared with desire as her voice grew soft and sensuous. "Do you want to verbally spar with me or would you like to do something else?"

His voice grew deep with desire. "Definitely something else."

A smile lifted her lips. "I thought so." She

tossed aside the blanket before pushing him back on the couch. "I have one request."

His heart was pounding. This was really going to happen. Christmas had come early for him. "Anything."

"Just don't let me turn into a pumpkin."

"Your wish is my command." He reached for his phone on the coffee table. He was in such a rush that he accidentally knocked it to the floor. With Gisella on top of him, he blindly fumbled around until his fingers came in contact with the phone. A few swipes later, he tossed it aside. "Your alarm is set."

She lowered her head to his, smothering his last word. After that all logical thoughts were lost to a scorching haze of desire for the Princess who had him seeing the holidays in a totally new light.

In the glow of the Christmas tree lights, they kissed. His lips moved over hers. Her mouth opened to him and his tongue delved inside, exploring and savoring the moment. Wrapped up in each other, he'd never been so content.

He knew the likelihood of them ever having a moment like this again was nil. He wanted to make sure she enjoyed every single moment of their lovemaking. And so, he took his time, refusing to rush. It was the sweetest torture with the most amazing ending. He'd never made love like that before.

There was something very special about Gisella. He had a feeling he'd never meet anyone who made him want to be a better person—want to put her feelings above the welfare of his company.

And now it was all about to end. He didn't have any regrets, except one. He wished there was a way they could spend more time together.

CHAPTER ELEVEN

She shouldn't have done it.

And yet she didn't regret one single kiss or caress.

Friday morning, Gisella couldn't help but smile. Her thoughts were full of memories of her evening with Silas. It had been magical. It was a date she'd never experienced before because it wasn't about being seen or shaking the right hands.

The evening had been all about them. It had been about enjoying themselves and having fun. And, oh, my, had she enjoyed herself. Silas had seen to it. Her cheeks were growing sore from all the smiling she was doing and she couldn't help it.

She strolled into the conference room at SC Public Relations a few minutes before eight with her staff in tow. She glanced around for Silas but didn't spot him. Disappointment assailed her.

"Good morning, Your Highness." She turned

to find Silas standing in the doorway. He bowed his head.

She wanted to tell him he didn't have to follow the royal protocols, but with their staff around them, she refrained. In truth, she didn't want to be treated like the future queen of Rydiania. She longed to be treated like Silas's friend—his very special friend. The smile pulled once more at the corners of her lips.

"You seem to be in a good mood this morning." Silas moved farther into the room.

"I am." She didn't see a need to deny it, but perhaps she needed to justify it. "It is a relief to have the planning for the gala almost wrapped up."

"I hope the planning wasn't too stressful." He moved to the head of the table and took a seat.

She sat to his left. "It wasn't. Thanks to you. It's been great working together."

"I agree."

They were saying all of the right things, but it felt to her as though they were talking in code about the time they spent outside of the office. And no one seemed to be the wiser. She couldn't help but wonder if the Duchess was in the room. She'd had her doubt about the spy being so close to her, but this trip had her reconsidering just how close the Duchess was to the royal family.

As though Silas had read her thoughts, he

said, "Did you see you made the headlines on *Duchess Tales* again?"

She rolled her eyes. She wanted to say that she didn't care what they'd printed. She refused to let them ruin her happiness.

"You might want to read it." Silas reached for his phone and pulled up the site.

It would be rude of her to reject his offer. And with the way he was pushing the subject, she worried that the Duchess had trash-talked her or, worse, she'd somehow figured out that they'd made love last night. As soon as the thought crossed her mind, she banished it. There was absolutely no way they could know what had gone down between her and Silas. It was a secret that would remain between them.

As she accepted Silas's phone, she wondered what fresh lies they'd printed this time. The horrid site seemed to have insights into her life that no one on the outside should have. Had she been spotted entering Silas's penthouse again? Or was it another moment during their date? There were quite a few people on top of the Empire State Building. Perhaps they'd taken their photo and sold it.

As soon as she realized her imagination was spiraling out of control, she halted it. Since when did she panic? She was usually the sibling that kept her cool, but when it came to this thing between her and Silas, she was acting out of character.

When she accepted the phone, their fingers touched. A jolt raced up her arm and sent her heart pitter-pattering. She forced her attention on the screen instead of the crazy sensations that Silas evoked within her.

TO DATE A PRINCESS

The breath caught in the back of Gisella's throat. She should have known they'd make a big deal of her evening with Silas. She hated how accurate the headline was, only because she wanted to keep the amazing evening to herself. She didn't want the gossip site to make up lies about it.

Beneath the headline was a photo of her and Silas entering Radio City Music Hall. She was smiling and so was he. They looked as if they didn't know their picture was being taken and that's because they hadn't known.

And as lovely as the picture was, she couldn't help but feel exposed. Anyone else who'd attended the theater that evening hadn't been noticed, but she'd gone and somehow it was world news. She'd wanted to fly under the radar and keep her time with Silas to herself.

Royal-watchers! Wait until you hear this. It appears our Crown Princess has found a romantic interest. Silas Cabot owns SC Public Relations. This is how they met...at least I don't think they knew each other before they started working on the Bee Global gala.

The question now is... Where does this leave Prince Matis? Oh, my. Does this mean their rumored impending marriage is off? What exactly is Princess Gisella thinking?

I wish I could tell you.

Gisella hated that the Duchess was putting doubts in people's minds about her decisions. This went beyond just bad press. The Duchess was out to undermine her reign. The Duchess had to be caught and stopped.

And what will Prince Matis's response be to all of this? Will he just walk away? Or will he fight for his princess?

I don't know, but it's gearing up to be a royal battle of the hearts.

Keep reading, my lovely watchers, and I'll share all of the messy details.

Until next time...

Duchess

She handed Silas's phone back to him with an

exasperated sigh. "She's certainly busy whipping up the public with her lies."

"Does this mean you aren't marrying the Prince guy?"

She sensed Silas wanted her to tell him that the marriage was a lie too. She swallowed hard. "That's the part they got right."

He frowned. "What's the Prince like?"

She shrugged. "He's okay."

"If you're going to marry the guy, shouldn't he be better than okay?"

"Honestly I don't know him very well." When she saw the confused look on Silas's face, she said, "Our parents are friends. They arranged the marriage in order to form an alliance between our kingdoms."

"So it's all politically motivated?"

She nodded. "It's my duty to marry him and strengthen our kingdom's political position on the global stage."

"But you don't want to marry him?"

"It doesn't matter what I want."

"You didn't answer the question. Do you want to marry the Prince?"

"No." It was the first time she admitted it to herself or anyone else.

She refused to let her worries about the future steal away her joy in the moment. This whole conversation was the Duchess's fault. When she returned to Rydiania, she planned to make un-covering the Duchess her main priority. Enough was enough.

"Let's get back to work."

He arched a questioning brow. "Are you sure you're up for it?"

She straightened her shoulders. "Of course I am. I'm not going to let the Duchess slow me down. Her day is coming, but today is all about the gala."

He smiled at her. "Okay, then. Let's get this meeting started."

And so their staffs sat down at the long table. They slowly went down over the long list of items for the gala, stopping with each one to discuss any potential problems. It was a slow process but a necessary one.

With her mind focused on the gala, her good mood returned. Even when there was a mix-up with the linens they'd requested, she maintained her optimism.

The linens that were supposed to be white were now a deep cherry red. They spoke with the florist and though it was too late to switch flowers to complement the linens, they merely left out the bright red mums. And now the ar-rangements were white and green. Nothing would clash. Thankfully.

Her mind kept spiraling back to the most

delish evening with Silas. She didn't know she could feel that alive and happy in a man's arms. He'd shown her what it was to be cherished and she just didn't know how she would ever be able to settle for anything less.

Sometimes a woman had to do what she had to do.

This was one of those times.

Gisella had spent the weekend sneaking around in order to meet Silas at his penthouse. On Saturday, she used the excuse of having an afternoon rendezvous that turned into dinner. And on Sunday evening, she'd pleaded a headache, only to slip away to Silas's place.

She couldn't believe she'd gotten away with it. She'd never done anything like it. But the more time she spent with Silas, the more time she wanted to spend with him. Their time together had been so wonderful and at the same time, it was bittersweet because this could only be a brief moment in time.

With Silas's encouragement, she had been able to experience a true sense of freedom and the sweetest affection before duty called to her. She would never regret giving up her virginity to Silas as he made her feel so special. Their time together would be a treasured memory that she would cling to as she reigned over Rydiania.

And on Monday afternoon after a productive morning, Gisella had returned to her hotel suite. Silas had some other business to attend to and she needed to address some royal matters.

But her progress was slow. She kept getting distracted with thoughts of Silas. He made her feel things she'd never felt before. And the memories they'd created together were locked away in her heart. They would never leave her.

But the thought of leaving Silas the day after tomorrow made her very sad. Sure, she wanted to be with her family for the holidays, but she also wanted to be with Silas. Maybe she could invite him to Rydiania for the holidays?

The thought appealed to her. What would be better than sharing Christmas morning with Silas? She'd simply tell her family that they'd become good friends while working on the gala. It was no big deal. And when he'd shown an interest in her country, she'd invited him for a visit. They had plenty of visitors to the palace on a regular basis. But none of them made her heart skip a beat.

"Your Royal Highness." Stephanie bowed her head before approaching her in the sitting room of Gisella's suite. "The correspondence has been sent by diplomatic pouch. I have today's papers for you to review. And your dress for the gala has been pressed."

"Thank you. I appreciate your help."

"Is there anything else I can do you for?"

"Not at the moment."

Stephanie turned and walked away. Even though they'd been working closely together this entire trip, Gisella still felt as though she didn't really know the woman. And she also got the feeling Stephanie didn't like her that much, which made her wonder if Stephanie was the Duchess. It would explain how she got all of that information.

And yet wouldn't her father's team have dug up some damaging information on Stephanie by now? Surely no one could be that cunning to cover up everything, could they?

Buzz.

She glanced at the caller ID on her phone. It was the palace. Perhaps there was finally news on the identity of the Duchess.

She pressed the phone to her ear. "This is Princess Gisella."

"Your Royal Highness, please hold for the Queen."

A few moments later, her mother came on the line. "Gisella, how is the gala coming?"

Her thoughts immediately went to the mix-up with the linens, but there was no reason to mention it since it had been easily resolved. "It's going well. It's been a lot of work but I think it's all going to pay off."

"Good. And then you'll be home just in time for Christmas."

"Yes, I will." It would also mean saying goodbye to Silas—unless she convinced him to come home with her—as a friend, of course. "And I was thinking we should invite some people to the palace to share the holidays with us."

"It was my thought too."

Gisella was caught off guard. Her mother wasn't usually so agreeable. She grew suspicious. What was her mother up to?

"Who do you intend to invite?" Gisella asked.

"I was thinking you might like to invite Matis."

Her heart stilled in her chest. For the past couple of days, Matis had been far from her thoughts. And now reality had come roaring back to her.

Thankfully her mother rushed on in her exuberance. "In fact, I was speaking with Matis's mother the other day." It didn't go unnoticed by Gisella that her mother made this conversation sound so incidental when in fact nothing the Queen did was by accident. "And she said Matis had some free time over the holidays. So, he's flying to New York to escort you to the gala. Isn't that perfect?"

Her mother sounded so pleased with her meddling. When in fact her mother's news arrowed into Gisella's chest, deflating all of her hopes that the gala would be an amazing night with Silas. Instead, she would have to pretend that she was enjoying Matis's company when in fact all she'd want to do was be with Silas.

"Gisella?" Her mother's voice drew her from her thoughts.

"Yes." She forced herself to sound happy about this news. "It's great news. I look forward to it."

"Gisella, is something wrong?"

Her eyes misted with unshed tears. She blinked them away. "Why would anything be wrong?"

Other than the little bit of happiness she'd found for herself was about to be stolen away. She'd joked with Silas about her turning into a pumpkin at midnight but it seemed the joke was on her because come the time of the gala she would indeed turn into a pumpkin.

But nothing could steal away the joyful memories she'd created with Silas. They would have to be enough to keep her company when her duties dictated that she marry someone who was a practical stranger to her—someone that she didn't love.

"You haven't forgotten about your responsibilities, have you?" There was a worried tone to her mother's words.

"No. I haven't." Maybe for a moment there she'd let herself imagine how life might be if she wasn't the Crown Princess. "I'll make sure Matis knows how much I appreciate him attending the gala with me."

"Very well."

And now she had to tell Silas that their plans to attend the gala together wouldn't happen. It was the last thing she wanted to do, but she had no choice. The responsibility of a queen was to do what was right for her kingdom—not what was right for her. Her needs had to come second—even if it was painful.

CHAPTER TWELVE

He sensed something was wrong.

Silas sat across from Gisella at dinner. They'd ventured out in public. He'd offered to take her to one of the trendy restaurants in Manhattan, but she'd declined. Instead, he'd taken her to Reagan's Bistro. It was a quiet, little family-run restaurant. Silas frequented it often. All of the employees knew his name and he had a regular table in the back.

He couldn't help but notice that Gisella was subdued. She'd barely touched her food. She made a pretense of moving it around on her plate but very little of it made it into her mouth.

It wasn't like her not to eat. Did she have regrets about getting involved with him because he wasn't a prince? After Gisella had told him about Prince Matis, he'd looked him up online.

The Prince was decent enough looking, but in almost every photo, he had a different woman on his arm. Was he some sort of royal playboy? Did Gisella know this about him? Did she care?

He couldn't imagine straying if he was fortunate enough to have Gisella as his bride. The thought startled him. Not that he was planning to marry her or anyone.

He gave himself a mental shake. None of this was any of his business. They'd both agreed to a no-strings fling. Nothing more. He couldn't change the rules now—even if he might want something more.

Maybe she wasn't even thinking about the Prince. And if that was the case, he certainly wasn't going to bring up the other guy.

Perhaps she was worried about the upcoming gala. He knew how much they both had riding on the success of the event. Yes, that must be it.

He cleared his throat. "If you're worried about the gala, don't be. I think we have all of the problems ironed out."

She shook her head. "I'm not worried." Her gaze met his. "You know you've been really great about everything. I appreciate all of your help."

"Then why don't you seem happy?"

"I am." She smiled but it didn't reach her eyes.

Instead of happiness, he only saw sadness. And then he realized that she was already worrying about leaving. He had to admit that her departure was quickly approaching. They had precious little time together and then she'd be jetting back to her far-off kingdom.

"I can't believe the gala is almost here." He reached out, placing his hand over hers and giving it a squeeze. "But we'll make the most of the time we have left together."

Before she could say anything, the server returned. She pulled her hand away. The server cleared their dishes, including Gisella's uneaten dinner.

She pulled out her phone and checked the time. "We should probably go."

He noticed she averted her gaze. "Would you like to go back to my place for some coffee or Christmas cookies?"

She shook her head. "I have a lot to do tonight. With all of the work on the gala, I've gotten behind on my other duties."

She was brushing him off? His ego was pricked. He wasn't used to being rejected. It was usually him that was the one to end things.

"I know you must have things to do." She slid her purse strap over her shoulder. "My bodyguards can give me a ride back to the hotel."

She wasn't just slowing things down, she was slamming on the brakes. Hard. And he felt as though he'd just gotten whiplash. Earlier in the day they'd been laughing and whispering among themselves. And now she couldn't get away from him fast enough.

"Gisella, what's going on?"

"Uh…nothing." She didn't look at him. "It's just that I'm tired and would like to get some rest. Good night." She got to her feet.

He rushed to stand in front of her. "Talk to me."

She stared at the ground. "I am."

"You're telling me everything except what's bothering you. Why are you so anxious to get out the door? Are you bored of me already?"

Her gaze darted up to meet his. "That's not true."

"Yes, it is. First, you barely talk. And then you don't eat your dinner. And now you're anxious to go back to your hotel alone."

"What do you want from me?" Her voice came out loudly.

Heads turned in their direction. The last thing they needed was to make a scene this close to the gala.

"Let's sit down." He gestured to their booth. "Please."

She sighed and then sat back down. He did the same. When the server returned, he ordered them some coffee.

"My mother always said these conversations were best done over something to drink." He sent her a reassuring smile that he didn't feel.

The server returned with fresh cups and a steaming pot of coffee. Gisella added creamer and sugar to hers. He left his black.

"Now, what's going on?" When he reached out to her, she pulled her hand away and placed it in her lap. "Gisella, I don't understand."

Her gaze met his. "I can't go to the gala with you."

He leaned back as though her words had smacked him in the face. He didn't know why this surprised him. She'd been pulling away from him all evening. It was obvious she had regrets about their fling.

The coffee sloshed nauseatingly in his stomach. He should say something now but he couldn't figure out an appropriate response. He was starting to feel as though she saw him as not good enough to be presented at the televised gala.

He'd been banking on them arriving at the gala together and spending the evening in each other's company. He'd already told Carl, the businessman he was negotiating the merger with, that he would be escorting Gisella. How was he going to explain this?

The awkward silence stretched on. He regretted pushing this conversation. Now he was trying to figure out a way to fix things—to convince her to still go to the gala with him.

"Whatever is wrong I'm sure we can fix it. Just tell me what I did."

"This isn't about you," she said.

"It sure feels that way," he muttered.

"I just found out that I'll be attending the gala with someone else."

His interest was piqued. He didn't like the thought of being replaced. "Who is this person?"

She shook her head. "It doesn't matter."

"It does to me."

She sighed. "It's Prince Matis."

He knew the name all too well. His gut twisted with an unusual burning sensation. "You mean the guy you're supposed to marry?"

She glanced down at her cup. "Yes."

He needed to know more. He couldn't help himself. "He's here? In New York?"

"Not yet but he will be soon."

Silas rubbed the back of his neck before his gaze met hers once more. "Do you love him?"

"What? No. Of course not. I hardly even know him."

"And yet you're planning to go through with the marriage?"

Her gaze narrowed. "Why are you acting like this? I have to marry him. It's not like I have a choice in this. And why do you care? This was supposed to be casual. Remember? No strings attached."

His back teeth ground together. He hated having his words thrown back in his face. "I remember. But we also had an agreement to go to the gala together."

"What are you saying?" Her gaze narrowed. "You want me to stand up Matis after he traveled all that way?"

That's exactly what he wanted her to do. He told himself that he was pushing the subject because he was attempting to protect his company and the pending merger.

"He'll understand that you had a prior commitment."

She rolled her eyes. "That's not going to happen."

"So that's it? You're blowing me off instead?"

She frowned at him. "That's not how I'd put it, but yes, I'm going to the gala with Matis." She got to her feet. "I'm sorry things ended this way."

When she walked away, he didn't stop her. His hand smacked the tabletop, rattling the flatware and making the coffee in his cup slosh against the sides.

He sat there for a while longer wondering if he had some royal blood in him if things would have gone different. In the back of his mind, he could still hear the echo of his father's voice saying, *"You aren't good enough."*

CHAPTER THIRTEEN

IT WAS COMING to an end.

Tomorrow was the gala.

Gisella's stomach knotted up at the thought of saying goodbye to Silas. It was the very last thing she wanted to do. And yet she didn't have a choice.

The past couple of weeks had been the longest and shortest of her life. She felt as though she'd learned a lot about herself. In fact, she no longer felt like the same person. The acknowledgment was profound for her.

Silas had helped her spread her wings. She'd learned to believe in her own judgment—to believe in herself. He'd shown her what it was like to relax and enjoy herself. She'd promised herself not to take life so seriously all of the time.

And now everything was coming to an end. She would miss this fun and adventurous city. Soon she'd be jetting back to Rydiania confident that she could be the queen her kingdom needed.

But she'd also be leaving Silas behind.

The thought stabbed at her heart. She'd done exactly what she'd told herself she wouldn't do—let herself care about Silas. And he was not someone she would easily get over.

"Your Royal Highness."

Gisella glanced up from her laptop that she'd been working on all morning. There were a lot of reports for her to stay on top of now that she was gearing up to be crowned queen in the new year. It was important that she knew everything that was going on back home while she would be making important connections on behalf of Rydiania with representatives from other countries at the gala.

"What is it?"

Her bodyguard Vic stood there in a dark gray suit and tie. His hands were clasped in front of him. "Prince Matis is here."

"Here? Already?"

Vic nodded his head. "Should I let him in?"

She glanced down at the email she was writing to the King. A warning flashed on the screen about a low battery. It would have to wait until later. She closed the laptop and set it aside.

"Give me two minutes." She jumped to her feet and moved to her room.

As she touched up her makeup and brushed her long hair, she told herself that she should be happy to see him. She wasn't. She wished it was Silas who was there to spend time with her. And she knew that was wrong. Matis was to be her future husband and yet she couldn't work up the appropriate excitement.

She hadn't seen Matis in months. She hoped that when her gaze settled on him that she would feel something. She needed to know that there was hope for her future marriage—that it would be more than a business arrangement.

She entered the sitting room to find Matis standing there. He was tall with dark hair and olive skin. He was easy enough on the eyes.

"Your Majesty." He bowed to her.

When he straightened and their gazes finally met, she waited for her heart to skip a beat as it did with Silas. She waited for her pulse to race. She waited for any sort of reaction to Matis's presence. And yet there was nothing.

"Hello, Matis. It's good to see you again."

"You look radiant, as always."

It was the voice she was going to hear the rest of her life. There was nothing she could do to change it. And yet she found herself struggling to accept this eventual union.

But she couldn't let him see her reservations. It was drilled into a princess from an early age to hide their feelings. They were trained to be able to smile under most circumstances. She presented him with one of her well-rehearsed smiles.

Matis was handsome—not as handsome as Silas, but good-looking in his own right. He was also easy to talk to. And he was to be her husband. It had been planned out since her brother stepped out of line for the throne.

Everything in her life had changed the day her brother put love ahead of his duty. And while she'd thought she was prepared to accept sacrificing her desires as she took on the duty of the crown, she was finding it increasingly difficult.

Silas had shown her another way to live—to follow her heart. And now she didn't know how to commit herself to a marriage where there was no love. She barely even knew Matis. And though some women would be thrilled with the prospect of marrying a handsome and charming prince, she wasn't. And it wasn't Matis's fault.

"Matis, you didn't have to come all this way for the gala."

He frowned. "You don't sound happy about me being here." Matis approached her. "Did I misunderstand what your mother was telling me?"

"I… I don't know what she told you." She hated when her mother went behind her back and tried to be a matchmaker.

"She said this was your biggest endeavor to date and it would mean a lot to you to have me here to support you. So here I am. But if I'm not wanted—"

"Of course you are." She forced a smile to her lips. She needed to accept the inevitable future and stop wishing for something that wasn't to be.

"Would you like to get some lunch?"

"I would but there's too many last-minute details that I need to stay on top of." She saw the disappointment flash in his eyes. She couldn't blame him. He'd traveled a long way to be here for her. "But you could pick me up at six o'clock for dinner."

He reached for her hand and kissed it. "Until later."

She watched him walk away. All the while she pondered his choice of words. Was he here out of duty? Was this whole arrangement between them a duty to him as well?

It was so hard to know because they didn't know each other well enough to talk about such intimate things. She was starting to realize that if they were going to be engaged in just a matter of days that they needed to have a serious conversation, but that was going to have to wait until later.

Right now, she needed to finish her work for

the King so that she could get on with reviewing the seating plans one final time.

She moved to the coffee nook and turned the carousel, searching for her favorite roast of coffee. There was none left. "Stephanie, do we have any more coffee pods?"

"Let me check." Stephanie moved to the counter and knelt down to open one of the doors. "There aren't any in here. I can call for more."

"Would you mind going to get them yourself?" Service in the hotel was slow. According to the hotel staff, they were shorthanded because of the holidays.

Her eyes momentarily widened, as though surprised to be asked to do something she deemed beneath her. "I'll get them."

After Stephanie left, both aides arrived for their one o'clock meeting. They intended to go over any last-minute details for the gala. So much for having lunch. Perhaps when Stephanie returned, they could order room service. Something told her if she didn't eat now, she wouldn't get to eat until dinner.

She and her two aides sat down at the long dining table in her suite. They started working down over their final checklists.

"Your Highness, would you like some coffee?" Eleanor asked.

"Go ahead. I ran out of my favorite blend. Stephanie went to get some more."

When Eleanor turned to Pearl, she said, "I'll have some French roast."

While Pearl joined Eleanor at the coffee nook, Gisella sat at the head of the table. She kept glancing at the time, knowing that it wouldn't be long until the hairstylist and makeup artist arrived to make her look camera ready for her dinner with Matis. It was likely to be a well-photographed affair.

Gisella opened her laptop and pulled up the email she was writing to the King. He might be her father but that didn't mean their correspondence was casual. It was all businesslike and straight to the point. In this case, she was weighing in on the possibility of a wind farm on palace lands. Her position was that they needed to do more investigating before agreeing to the venture.

"Where did you say Stephanie went for the coffee?" Pearl asked.

"Down to the front desk," Gisella answered. "I'm surprised she's not back yet."

"We're also out of the French roast and creamer. I'll go catch up with her." She turned for the door before pausing and turning back. "If that's all right with you, Your Highness."

"Yes. Of course. Just don't take too long. We

don't have much time before I have to prepare for dinner with Prince Matis."

Pearl nodded and headed out the door.

Gisella turned back to her computer. Her fingers moved rapidly over the keyboard as she typed out the questions she still had about the windmill farm. Her biggest concern was that even though the palace owned a great amount of land, the windmills would be too close to the palace because of the noise pollution as well as the danger posed to wildlife.

A message flashed on her screen, telling her that her battery was dead. And then the monitor went black. That was it. No other warning. And no chance for her to save her work.

She worried about how much of her well-thought-out words she'd lost. She groaned in frustration.

"Your Highness, is something wrong?" Eleanor sent her a worried look.

"My laptop died and I have an email I must finish."

"You could use my laptop."

Gisella shook her head. "You have to finish the verification of the guest list."

"I know. Use Pearl's. Her work laptop is at the other end of the table. She won't mind."

Gisella wasn't particularly worried since all of the computers were palace owned. And being the Crown Princess, she had sign-on authority for all palace computers except for the King's.

She logged on to the computer and moved to the email. She pulled up her partially completed email and was relieved that she'd only lost a couple of lines. She quickly retyped them.

Stephanie and Pearl walked in the room with a couple of boxes of coffee and some creamer.

Eleanor glanced up from her computer. "Hey, Pearl, the Princess borrowed your computer."

"What? Why?" She dropped her coffee on the chair and marched over to the Princess. "You can't do that." She snatched away the computer.

No one ever took things from Gisella. Not ever. And there was a look of panic in Pearl's eyes. Gisella sensed there was something terribly wrong here. It took her a minute to figure out what it might be.

Pearl clutched the laptop to her chest.

Stephanie placed her coffee supplies on the table. She glanced at Gisella with a wide-eyed stare as though to say that she had no idea what the outburst was about.

Stephanie stepped up to Pearl and held out her hands. "Hand over the computer."

"No. It's mine."

"You know that all computers are owned by the palace. The Princess has every right to use any of our work computers. And you also know not to do personal things on your work computer." When Pearl still didn't relinquish the computer, Stephanie's voice rose. "Hand it over. Now!"

As though Vic had heard the raised voices, he stepped into the suite. His guarded expression scanned the room and settled on the two women. "Is there a problem here?"

Gisella got to her feet and approached Pearl. "You're the Duchess, aren't you?"

Pearl continued to clutch the computer as she silently glared at Gisella. This was a side of Pearl she'd never seen before. There was pure hatred gleaming in her dark eyes.

It was in that moment that Gisella got all the confirmation she needed. Either Pearl was the Duchess or she'd been conspiring with the Duchess. It was the only way the Duchess could have received the information that had been recently printed.

Gisella did something she'd never done before. She straightened her shoulders, lifted her chin ever so slightly and held out her hand. "I command you to hand over the laptop."

Their gazes clashed. Gisella wouldn't look away. This felt like a test of the type of leader she would be for her country. She wanted to be compassionate and fair, but she also wanted people to respect her authority.

The whole room filled with a quiet tension. Everyone waited to see how this would play out. Gisella didn't want to call the rest of her security team to wrench the laptop from her, but if it came to that she would do it. The computer belonged to the realm.

Pearl thrust the computer at Gisella. "Take it. But it won't stop me."

Gisella accepted the laptop. "Take her to her room. She is to remain under guard until arrangements are made for her to be escorted back to Rydiania."

"You can't do anything to me," Pearl shouted. "There's freedom of speech!"

"There's also a nondisclosure agreement you signed before being hired by the palace. There's also spying on the royal family."

Pearl's face scrunched into a frown. "You won't silence me."

Two bodyguards escorted a now-shouting Pearl from the suite. Gisella took her first easy breath. She couldn't believe the spy had been a part of her staff, hiding in plain sight. If not for the trip to New York and her dead laptop battery, she wouldn't have caught on to what was happening right beneath her nose.

The first thing she did was reach for her phone and call Silas. She couldn't wait to tell him that the mystery of *The Duchess Tales* had been resolved. But as the phone continued to ring…and ring…she was beginning to think calling him was a mistake.

And then his deep voice filled the line. "Hello, Your Highness."

Just the sound of his voice caused a smile to lift the corners of her mouth. She loved the deep timbre of his voice. It was so warm and made her heart flutter. She couldn't help but notice the difference in her reactions to Silas and Matis.

"What may I do for you?" Silas's voice drew her from her thoughts.

"Actually, I have some news for you."

"I assume this about the gala."

"No, it's not."

"Then I need to go."

"No! Wait." She couldn't believe he was going to hang up on her. No one ever hung up on her. But there had never been anyone in her life like Silas. He didn't look at her like she was a princess, soon to be a queen. He looked at her like she was his equal. And it felt so good not to be put up on a pedestal that she was constantly struggling not to fall off.

He sighed. "There's nothing left to say. Goodbye."

"Silas?"

There was no response.

"Silas?"

Still there was nothing on his end. The line went dead.

That was it. He didn't even want to speak to her now. She knew she deserved it after their dinner the night before.

She hadn't handled things well with her real life intruding on her fling with Silas. She should have worked harder to hide her feelings from Silas, but she'd never felt like she had to put on a show for him. When they were together, she felt like she could be herself—something she'd never felt with anyone else—even with her siblings, who looked at her as the responsible one.

She assured herself that she would smooth things out with Silas at the gala, but she wondered if that was even possible. Reality had come crashing in on them and their fling was officially over. The thought sliced into her heart with a pain she'd never felt before.

CHAPTER FOURTEEN

Christmas was just a week away.

Later that day, Silas removed the sparkly ornaments from the tree in his living room. He didn't want the reminders of the time he'd spent with Gisella. Because as amazing as those moments had been, he was reminded that they could never happen again.

He told himself that once he removed all of the Christmas decorations and his penthouse returned to its sparse modern decor that he'd feel like himself again. He'd be able to focus one hundred percent on the merger that was so close to being official.

Once his business was expanded to the West Coast, he'd be too busy traveling between the numerous offices to think about Gisella. Memories of her would sink to the back of his mind. And all would be as it had once been.

Removing the ornaments took him a couple of hours. And then he'd had a couple of men remove the tree. He found the vacuum in the hall closest and swept up the pine needles.

He picked up the boxes of ornaments and carried them to the spare room. He'd worry about donating them the next day. But when he stepped into the room, he found the bed covered with the presents they'd bought for Mary and little Susie.

He'd totally forgotten about them. They were already wrapped and tagged. All they needed were to be delivered. He'd deal with them another time.

He turned and headed into the hallway. As he went to pull the door shut behind him, his gaze caught the presents again. They were one more thing to remind him of Gisella. He sighed.

He called up his car and had the presents as well as the ornaments put in the car. He would deliver them now and tomorrow when he returned from the gala, the apartment would be devoid of anything that reminded him of Gisella.

He had Mary's new address in his phone. It was on Staten Island not far from his mother's house. It wasn't until he was almost to the apartment that he realized he should have called ahead. If Mary wasn't home, he didn't want to leave all of the packages outside her door.

The car pulled up in front of the converted town house. Mary and Susie lived on the top floor. He climbed the steps and knocked on the door. He didn't hear any voices. He worried they weren't home, but then the door opened.

Mary smiled as soon as she saw him. "Hi."

"Hello. I have a few things for you and the baby. Would you mind if I brought them in?" When she glanced past him into the hallway, he said, "The Princess couldn't make it."

"That's too bad. You two make such a cute couple."

Really? He hadn't realized they gave off that impression. "Oh, we're not a couple."

"Could have fooled me. Did you get her something for Christmas?"

He shook his head. The truth of the matter was he hadn't thought of getting her a gift. "I'll get the packages."

In the light of a new day, he regretted his angry outburst the night before. He wondered if a present would be an acceptable peace offering. Perhaps if he were to get her something meaningful, she might forgive his outburst. Not that he thought they had a chance as a real couple. If they had a real relationship, it would mean he'd just been royally dumped. The thought didn't sit well with him.

With the help of his driver, it took them a couple of trips to carry up the gifts and decorations. Noticing they didn't have a Christmas tree, he called his assistant and arranged for one to be delivered later that day. His assistant seemed a bit surprised by the gesture. It must mean that Gisella had rubbed off on him.

Mary glanced at all of the Christmas presents. "Thank you so much for all of this. I don't know how I'll ever repay you."

"That's not necessary. And most of this was the Princess's idea."

"That was very sweet of her. Please thank her for me."

"Is the apartment working out?"

Mary smiled and nodded. "I like it here. We have great neighbors and there's a little park on the next block."

"I'm glad to hear it."

They made a little more small talk and then he was gone. But as they drove into Manhattan, he kept thinking about his conversation with Mary. Maybe she was right. Maybe he should get Gisella a Christmas present—just a little something to remind her of their time together.

The big day had finally arrived.

Gisella had hardly slept. The night had been filled with her tossing and turning. She told herself that she was anxious about the gala going perfectly so she could show her kingdom and the world that she would make a good ruler—

that she wasn't just the backup choice for the crown.

Except that deep inside she knew it was only partially true. The other part of her missed Silas. The frosty gap between them felt like Antarctica. And she knew it was her fault. She hadn't handled ending their fling very well.

She'd still been dealing with the news that Matis would be taking her to the gala instead of Silas. Her mother must have read those articles on *The Duchess Tales* site and believed them. Those posts had totally missed the mark.

There was no way she was falling in love with Silas. They were so different from each other, including their backgrounds. Besides, he wasn't falling for her. Nothing he said had made her think she'd wormed her way into his heart.

They'd had a holiday fling. Nothing more. And as good as it had been, it was over now. They'd both known this day was coming. It had simply arrived two days early.

She had to accept that her future had all been laid out for her. Now she had to step into the role and start living the life of a crown princess.

And so, she had taken great pains in her appearance that evening as it would be broadcast not only in the States but also in Rydiania. This was her one chance to show everyone the future of Rydiania would be safe under her supervision.

The Princess's suite was a flurry of activity. Her one remaining aide was surprisingly quiet though Eleanor did everything that was asked of her. However, Eleanor made a point of avoiding eye contact with the Princess.

When Eleanor departed on an errand, Gisella turned to Stephanie. "Do you know what's going on with her? She doesn't seem to be acting like herself."

"I wouldn't worry, ma'am. I think she's rattled by your discovery that Pearl is the Duchess and worried that you'll think she was involved with the ordeal."

Gisella had to admit that she'd been suspicious of both Eleanor and even Stephanie in the beginning. But palace security had worked with the Rydianian police overnight and this morning she'd received a call from the King, assuring her that Pearl had acted alone.

"Please reassure Eleanor that she has nothing to worry about."

Stephanie nodded. "I will, ma'am."

A phone rang and Stephanie stepped out of the room to take the call. Gisella was relieved for a moment to be alone to gather her thoughts. Tonight was the beginning of her new life. From here on out, everything would be proper. There would be no more vicious lies from *The Duchess Tales*. And there would be no room for romantic romps. Everything would be serious and done according to protocol. Why did that suddenly sound like a life sentence to her?

She'd been so certain her entire life that if given a chance, she wanted to be queen. And now suddenly she was having second thoughts. Did she really regret wishing for a chance to step up and take the crown? Her answer was an immediate no. It was all of the other stuff that she wasn't thrilled about—like marrying someone she didn't care about and then producing a family with him. But it was too late to change any of it now. The die had been cast. And she had a prince arriving to escort her to the gala.

She glanced in the mirror at the sleeveless designer gown. The silver material was studded with seed beads that shimmered in the light. Her hair had been drawn up with a few curls around her neck. A diamond-studded tiara had been placed just so in her hair and secured.

Next, she was helped on with a pair of black evening gloves. And then she was ready to put on a big smile in order to greet this evening's guests. It was going to be a busy night. Maybe she'd be too busy to notice that Silas wasn't at her side.

She knew that wasn't going to happen. The memory of Silas was in everything about the evening, even down to the red linens on the table.

After the mix-up with the linen colors, they'd worked together to change the dishes to a simple white and the flower arrangements were adjusted so the whole table setup would flow seamlessly together.

Knock-knock.

Gisella gave her appearance one last glance. "Come in."

Stephanie stepped inside the room, closing the door behind her. "Your Royal Highness," she briefly curtsied. "Prince Matis has arrived."

"I'm coming." She slipped her feet into a pair of black heels. She grabbed a black clutch purse from a table and made her way out of the room.

When he approached her, her heart leaped into her throat. Was he planning to kiss her? Surely not. She quickly outstretched her gloved hand to him. Surprise shone in his eyes. Wordlessly he took her hand and kissed it.

What was wrong with her? How was it that the man she was expected to marry she didn't even want to kiss? She inwardly groaned. This was going to be so much harder than she ever imagined.

When he pulled back, she took her first easy breath. "Are you ready to go?"

His brows rose. "Already?"

"I must arrive early to see to some final details."

He sat down on one of the white couches and

pulled out his phone. With his attention on the phone's screen, he said, "Won't your staff see to such things?"

Her back teeth ground. When she'd mentioned the gala at last night's dinner, he'd changed the subject. She'd told herself that his lack of interest was due to jet lag. She couldn't use that excuse for his behavior today.

"I really need to leave," she said.

"There's no need to rush. You're going to be queen. You have to get used to delegating these sorts of things to your staff."

She didn't like how he dismissed her words and acted as though she didn't truly have things to do. She was seeing a side of Matis that she hadn't seen before.

Or was it possible she'd overlooked these things in the past? But now that Silas had entered her life, she had someone to compare Matis to—someone who supported her and her efforts. And Matis failed in comparison.

"I'm sorry if my mother misrepresented the event, but I am hosting tonight's gala. I need to be there early to make sure everything is running smoothly. If you would like to wait here until later this evening, I'll make sure my staff makes you comfortable." She started for the door.

A moment later, Matis was by her side. "I'll

escort you there. I just hope you aren't wasting your time."

Was Matis always this irritating? Or was she really that blind to it? Either way, how were they going to find a way to coexist in a marriage of convenience?

CHAPTER FIFTEEN

THINGS COULDN'T END this way.

Silas paced in the Great Hall of the Metropolitan Museum of Art. He'd escorted his mother to the party. She was meandering around taking in the art. They'd arrived early so he could make sure everything was in place for this evening's big event.

Silas forked his fingers through his hair, not caring if he messed it up. He was angry at himself for letting this fling with Gisella get out of control. Yet through it all, he didn't think it was all one-sided. Gisella had acted as though she'd really enjoyed their time together.

He thought back to their Christmas shopping and a smile threatened to pull at his lips, but he resisted the urge. Come tomorrow Gisella would be stepping on a private jet and flying back to Rydiania. He would never see her again.

And yet he knew that's the way it had to be because try as he might, he just wasn't cut out to be Gisella's husband—he wasn't of royal blood. Gisella had made it perfectly clear that she had to abide by royal protocol and her kingdom's charter. It all conspired to leave him out of her life. He could hear his father's words echoing in his mind—*"You aren't good enough."*

His hands clenched. He'd come so far in life and yet he hadn't come as far as he'd thought. But it wasn't like it was serious between them. They'd gone into this relationship with their eyes open. There had been no promises of anything more. There had been no expectations. And there had been clarity that when this evening ended, so did they.

Silas strolled through the American Wing. He hoped to catch Gisella before the gala moved into full swing. He didn't want things between them to end with the angry words they'd shared the other evening. He wanted her to hang on to the good memories and that's why he got her a little gift.

When a hush fell over the room, it drew his attention. He stopped and turned. His gaze followed everyone else's to the door. And there stood Gisella.

He struggled to keep his mouth from gaping. She was no longer the sweet and fun Gisella that had accompanied him around Manhattan for the past couple of weeks. She had transformed into a genuine princess.

She stood tall with her shoulders drawn back. Her long brown curls were drawn up except for a few wispy curls around the nape of her slender neck. A sparkling tiara rested on her head. She carried it as naturally as some people wore hairbands.

The silver gown exposed her shoulders and the neckline delved down just enough to give the briefest hint of her cleavage. The long dress hugged her luscious curves.

He longed to tell her how beautiful he found her. Before he knew what he was doing, he started in her direction. It wasn't until he was halfway across the room that common sense kicked in.

He stopped. He couldn't go to her now. Beyond her bodyguards there was another man standing at her side. This must be Prince Matis.

The man was frowning as he spoke to Gisella. Silas wondered what was being said, not that it was any of his business. Gisella had made it clear that their fling was over. It was her life—her choices. Not that it made him feel any better.

Standing there staring at Gisella certainly wasn't going to help his mood. He turned and moved backstage. He didn't have a destination in mind, but he quickly found himself caught up in a discussion with the sound guy. He welcomed a distraction from his thoughts of Gisella with that prince guy.

He should be relieved that Gisella wasn't taking up his time. He should be focusing on impressing Mr. Carr. Tonight was his chance to impress the West Coast company and show them why they would work well together. They would be able to take on accounts that required marketing from coast to coast.

And for all of the reasons it was good that the fling with the Princess was over, he found himself thinking of how much he would miss her. Everything reminded him of her. This whole evening had her fingerprints all over it.

The gala got underway. The Princess gave a brief welcoming speech. Dinner was served. Silas was seated between his mother and Mr. Carr. As he stared down at his plate of food, he found that he'd lost his appetite. This was going to be the longest evening of his entire life.

After the dessert was served, the awards were handed out for the most innovative research into preserving bees and helping them to flourish. The winners were from Rydiania, the United States and Australia. And to Silas's relief, the show had gone off without a hitch.

"I'm impressed." The male voice came from his side.

Silas turned to find Carl Carr with a pleased look on his face. The man had short silver hair, a trim figure and an authoritative presence. He owned West Coast PR.

Immediately a smile lifted the corners of Silas's mouth. "I'm so glad to hear that."

"The success of this gala makes me appreciate your company all the more," Carl said. "It has alleviated my worries. You do realize my company has been my life's work. Letting it go is difficult for me."

Silas nodded. "I can understand that. I feel the same way about my company."

"If I was ten years younger this conversation might be the other way around."

"I can imagine." Though there was no way Silas would sell his company. It was a part of him. It grounded him and gave him a reason to get out of bed in the morning.

Carl cleared his throat. "Would you mind introducing me to the Princess?"

Silas didn't want to go over to where she was standing next to the Prince and laughing at something he said. The thought of making nice with them would kill him on the inside, but when he glanced over at Carl, who sent him an expectant look, he knew he didn't have any choice if he wanted this merger to go through.

"Sure. Come on." His feet felt as though they

weighed a couple of hundred pounds each as he made his way through the fashionably dressed crowd.

They had to wait a moment while Gisella finished speaking to an older couple. When the people stepped away, Gisella's eyes briefly widened when she noticed him. So, she hadn't expected him to approach her tonight, which told him that if it wasn't for Carl, they would have spent the remainder of the evening ignoring each other.

Gisella, being the proper princess, put on a smile as Silas briefly bowed his head to her.

Prince Matis didn't say much. Carl complimented the Princess about the gala. When the conversation dwindled, Carl excused himself to take a phone call. Silas wasn't sure that the man's phone really rang because he hadn't heard anything or if Carl just couldn't think of anything else to say.

Silas knew he should move on but once again his feet just weren't cooperating. The truth was he missed Gisella's company. When he was with her, life seemed so much brighter.

Prince Matis cleared his throat. "You did a fine job with the gala."

His compliment surprised Silas. He wanted to dislike the guy, but so far, he hadn't been bad. "Thank you. But Gisella deserves most of the credit. She worked hard to make sure all of the details were attended to."

"Soon she won't have to worry about things like this," Matis said. "She'll have other matters to attend to—like our wedding."

The boldness of his statement caught Silas off guard. His gaze immediately moved to Gisella, who glanced away. He looked at Matis once more. "Congratulations." He mustered all of his determination in order to act indifferent and shake the man's hand. "I should make the rounds."

He turned and walked away. He didn't know why Gisella's impending marriage to *this guy* should feel like a gut punch. It wasn't like they'd gone into their relationship with any expectations. And she did tell him that when she married it had to be to someone of royal descent.

He had no interest in speaking with anyone. His gaze moved to the closest exit. But he couldn't just disappear. His mother was around here somewhere and he needed to see her home. He was stuck.

"Silas, wait." Gisella's voice came from behind him.

He kept walking. He had no direction in mind, but he didn't want to speak to her. Not now. A hand reached out, touching his arm.

He stopped and turned. "Gisella, we have nothing left to say."

"I disagree."

"Shouldn't you be with your fiancé?"

"Silas, this isn't my choice. You have to understand that my life has been dictated to me since I was a little girl."

He believed her, but it didn't make him feel the least bit better. "You don't have to explain it to me." He turned to walk away.

"Yes, I do!"

The urgency of her voice had him turning back. He found that he wasn't the only one who had turned to look at the Princess. It appeared they'd gained an audience.

Apparently Gisella noticed as well. "Dance with me?"

He shook his head. "It's not a good idea."

She lowered her voice. "Why are you being like this? Is it because of how I acted yesterday?" She looked at him expectantly. When he didn't answer, she said, "I'm sorry. When I talked to my mother and she told me Matis was on his way, I was reminded of my life and responsibilities."

"You don't have to apologize. We both knew when we started this thing that it was going to end. Now I need to be going."

"Wait." Her eyes begged him to agree. "I have news."

When he didn't move, she told him about

catching the Duchess. It was so hard to believe that the spy had gotten so close to Gisella. He hoped they would improve their security and screening process so this never happened again.

Before he could respond, Matis joined them. The Prince's gaze met his. "Do you mind if I steal her away?"

Silas's gaze returned to Gisella's. "Not at all. We're finished."

They were the two hardest words for him to say. He should have known better than to have a fling with a princess. His father would tell him that once again he wasn't good enough—not royal enough—not royal at all.

It wasn't until Gisella and Matis walked away that he realized he didn't want things to end this way. He still had the Christmas present he'd bought her in his pocket. Maybe he'd find a moment to give it to her later. Then again, maybe it was best that he didn't give it to her at all. He was so torn.

The gala had been a huge success.

Well…sort of.

The next morning, Gisella still couldn't forget the way Silas looked at her when she was with Matis. The look in his eyes was like one of betrayal. She'd wanted to go to him and explain to him that what she had with Matis was nothing like what she had with him. Not even close.

Her relationship with Matis was a business arrangement. The thing she had with Silas was anything but business. It was exciting, exhilarating and addictive. How was she going to live without that sort of relationship in her life?

It was like her life took on Technicolor when Silas was in it. And now with Silas gone, her life had returned to a black-and-white existence. She had no idea what to do about that.

All morning, her phone had rung. She'd heard from the Queen, who had praised the gala and said that she'd wished she could have been there. Gisella also heard from future gala sponsors from France, Germany and South Africa. The Bee Global program was growing exponentially. It was even more impressive than its inaugural gala under her father's guidance. That knowledge bolstered her that her path in life was the correct one—even if the sacrifices to walk this path were staggering.

And now on her flight home, the King called. He'd praised the gala and told her that she and Matis made a good-looking couple. Eventually the conversation moved on to the person behind *The Duchess Tales*.

"I can't believe Pearl was so brazen to have

used a palace laptop," Gisella said. "If not for that mistake, we might still not have caught her."

"I think it was a mix of her thinking she was smarter than everyone else and being restricted on what she could take on the trip."

"Why couldn't we figure out that Pearl was behind *The Duchess Tales*?" Gisella asked her father.

"It turned out that she had stolen someone else's identity. That's why our background checks didn't turn up anything."

Gisella gasped at the audacity of Pearl or whoever she was. "And now that she's been caught that's another charge on top of spying on the royal family."

"Trust me, that's just half of it. Apparently, she's quite the con artist."

"How are we going to keep this from happening again?" She didn't want to have to be suspicious of everyone that worked in the palace.

"I don't know but I have our people working on new protocols for hiring royal staff. After Christmas I'd like you to head up those discussions."

It didn't go unnoticed by her that her father had said *our* people instead of my people. It meant that all of the Duchess's lies and innuendoes hadn't changed her father's mind about her stepping up as queen. His belief in her abilities had her mouth lifting at the corners.

"I'd be happy to."

"And there's another issue to address with the Duchess."

Her heart stilled.

Please don't let it be more bad news.

"What might that be?"

"It appears Pearl has amassed a rather substantial sum in various bank accounts. Once she's convicted of spying on the crown for a profit those funds will be confiscated. I'll need you to see that those funds are properly redistributed via the royal charities."

"I'd be happy to do that." Very happy indeed. At least something good would come from the awful affair.

A few minutes later, they wrapped up their conversation. She glanced around and found that Matis was still in the rear of the plane as he worked on his laptop. When their gazes met, he held up a finger to her.

A minute later, he once more sat in the seat next to her. When the flight attendant came to check on them, he said, "Can we have some champagne?"

The flight attendant nodded her head. "I'll be right back."

"Champagne?" Gisella wondered if Matis

drank it all of the time or if he was celebrating something. There were just so many things she didn't know about him. "What's up with that?"

He leaned back in the seat and crossed his legs by resting his foot on his knee. "I thought we should celebrate."

"Celebrate what?"

His gaze lifted to meet hers. "I figure news of our engagement will be released over Christmas, right? I mean, you still want to go through with it, don't you?"

Was that his version of a proposal? If so, it was awful. It only succeeded in confirming that he felt the same way about this marriage as she did.

Everything within her screamed that this was wrong. She didn't need to marry him in order to rule over Rydiania. In fact, she didn't need him at all. She wondered if he felt the same way about her.

"Matis, do you want to do this?"

"You mean get married?" When she nodded, he said, "It's what our parents want."

"I didn't ask about our parents. I'm asking what you want."

Before he could answer, the flight attendant returned with the champagne. They each took a glass but neither of them drank any. There was a strained silence between them as though Matis wasn't sure what he should say to her.

She honestly didn't know what she wanted him to say. There was a part of her that wanted to live up to her family's expectations, but there was another part of her that realized in order to be an effective queen, she needed to have the backbone to stand by her decisions, even when they made others unhappy.

She turned to him. "I can tell by your silence that this marriage isn't what you would choose for yourself. Is that fair to say?" When he nodded, she said, "It's not what I would choose either. I know life isn't always easy and you need someone by your side who's going to make those hard times a little easier. Someone that you want to come home to at the end of the day."

"And that's not me?"

She glanced away, but then she realized that she had to face her decisions—no matter how difficult they may be. Her gaze met his once more. "No. It's not."

His expression was devoid of emotion. "So, the engagement and wedding are off?"

She nodded. "To be honest, they were never on for anyone but our parents."

"Agreed." He held up his champagne flute to her and at last he smiled. "Here's to the future."

She lifted her glass. "May we both find happiness."

They clinked their glasses together and then took a sip of the bubbly liquid.

She didn't know what her future would be romantically, but she knew she couldn't commit herself to a loveless marriage. Now that she knew what a real relationship could be like, she couldn't accept less.

CHAPTER SIXTEEN

He'd never had this problem before.

He couldn't focus on work.

Even though the merger was commencing and this should be the highlight of his career, Silas wasn't happy. He was short-tempered and nothing felt right. His normally congenial assistant was now prone to frowning at him.

He raked his fingers through his hair. With a frustrated sigh, he leaned back in his chair. Why had he let himself get so close to Gisella? He never did that with anyone. And yet there was something about her that had him doing and saying things he didn't normally do.

It was the morning after the gala—the day Gisella had returned to Rydiania and Silas found himself climbing the walls. When his mother called and needed something from the store, he used it as an excuse to get out of the office. There was no one there he wanted to talk to and nothing that could occupy his mind.

And so, he picked up his mother's order and showed up at her house an hour later. When she opened the door, her eyes momentarily widened. "Silas, what are you doing here?"

He stepped inside out of the winter wind. "Didn't you say you needed some food?"

"Yes. But I didn't expect you to drop everything in order to get it for me."

He shrugged. "I had some time."

She led him to the kitchen, where she put away the groceries before pouring each of them a cup of coffee. When she joined him at the table, she said, "What has you so distracted?"

He shrugged again. "Nothing."

"Oh, Silas, you don't expect me to believe that, do you? It's because Gisella's gone, isn't it?"

His mother always could read him well. "She left because she had a country to run."

"Must be something being a genuine princess. I can't even imagine what that responsibility must be like."

He should say something, but he remained quiet as he stared at his black coffee, wondering what Gisella was up to right now. He wondered if she ever thought of him. Perhaps not since things didn't end on the best note. And that was his fault. He hadn't reacted well to seeing her with the Prince—the man she was supposed to marry.

"Silas, your coffee is getting cold." His mother's voice drew him from his thoughts. "Are you planning to talk? Or are you just going to sit there and scowl?"

His gaze rose to meet hers. "I'm not scowling."

His mother rolled her eyes as she shook her head. "You're thinking about Gisella, aren't you?"

"I am not."

Liar. Liar.

"I think I'm old enough to know when I see someone with a broken heart."

"It's not like that."

She arched a disbelieving brow. "I noticed that you got really close to Gisella while she was here, didn't you? It seemed like you were spending every minute of the day together."

He shrugged his shoulders. "She needed someone to show her around the city."

"And there wasn't anyone else willing to show her the sights but you?"

He wasn't so sure his mother needed his input. She seemed to have this conversation well under control. It didn't matter what he said, she was going to turn it all around on him. So, this time he didn't bother to answer her.

"Silas, I'm going to tell you something that you might not be willing to admit to yourself."

He stared at his full coffee cup as his gut

knotted up. He hated when his mother had one of her insightful moments.

"You're in love with her."

"No!" He pushed back his chair. He got to his feet and started to pace around the kitchen. "You have it all wrong. We were friends. Nothing more."

As though he hadn't said a word, his mother continued. "And I think she's in love with you too."

He leaned back against the counter and rubbed the back of his neck. "Why are you doing this?"

"Because someone has to make you see some sense. A love like that doesn't come around very often—sometimes not at all. If you waste this opportunity, you'll regret it."

He was so tired of his mother jumping to all of these conclusions. With an exasperated sigh, he said, "If Gisella was so in love with me, why did she leave?"

His mother took a moment to sip at her coffee. She turned to him. "I think you pushed her away."

She was right, but he wasn't ready to admit it to her or himself. "Why would you say that?"

"Because that's what you do when anyone gets too close to you. And I know it has to do with your father. He was too rough on you. I told him to stop, but he didn't listen to me. He never listened to anyone. I hope you aren't stubborn like him. I hope you'll listen to me. You need to go after Gisella and tell her how you feel."

"I can't. I don't fit into her world. I'm not royalty."

His mother stood and moved to him. "True love will find a way."

Deep down he wanted to believe her, but logically he knew it was impossible. And yet there was a part of him that just couldn't let go of her. Was there some possibility they'd both overlooked?

What would it hurt to go see her? To wish her a merry Christmas? And to give her the present he'd gotten her? After all, it was the time of the year when wishes really did come true.

"Thanks, Mom." He kissed her cheek before starting for the door.

"You're going to Rydiania?" There was a hopeful note in her voice.

He turned back. "I am. I just have to make a stop first."

A big smile covered his mother's face. "Go get the woman you love."

That's what he intended to do. Once he got her one more gift, he'd set off for Rydiania. He knew a future with Gisella wouldn't be easy. In fact, it was more like impossible. But he wasn't giving up. He thrived on challenges. And this was the most important challenge of his life.

She missed him.
She missed his smile.
She missed his deep rumbly laugh.
On her first evening home, Gisella stared out the window at the snowy sky. She wondered what Silas was doing at that moment. She wanted to phone him and tell him that she'd called off the prearranged marriage to Matis. Her parents had been furious about her decision, but then she'd told them that Matis didn't want to marry her either. It didn't make them happy but at least they stopped hounding her to fix things. They finally accepted that the relationship was irretrievably broken.

To say her homecoming had been stressful was an understatement. At least she no longer felt as though someone was watching over her shoulder. And thankfully there were no tabloid headlines about her and Silas. However, she and Matis formally going their own ways had made the headline news and rightly so. Her staff had released a proper announcement. The people of Rydiania needed to know that Matis wouldn't be marrying their future queen.

Gisella sat idly in her office a few days before Christmas. She hadn't gotten much done. Every time she started to read an email, she got distracted with thoughts of Silas. Then she'd forget what she had read and have to start all over at the beginning once more.

She missed Silas so much. She'd even called his office with the excuse of checking on some dishes that had been broken in a mishap with the waitstaff. To her great disappointment, he wasn't in the office. Instead, she spoke with his assistant, who was very nice but far from chatty.

If she wanted to know anything about Silas, it was up to her to ask. So as casually as she could she brought up the subject of the merger and how she'd met Silas's business associate at the gala. She asked if the merger was moving forward. His assistant confirmed that the merger was still on, but that's all she said. And Gisella didn't push the subject.

She was happy for Silas. This merger had been what he truly wanted and now it was happening. Both of them had bright futures. Although his future was on one continent while hers was a long way away on another continent.

Knock-knock.

The door opened and an aide announced that her sister would like to see her. Gisella eagerly welcomed the distraction. Cecelia and her husband had just arrived from the South of France to celebrate the holidays. It was going to be great to have the whole family together for Christmas.

Cecelia walked with a bit of a waddle. Her face had that expectant mother glow. Gisella wondered if she'd ever know that sort of happiness. Her chances of becoming a mother had shrunk considerably now that she'd ended things with Matis. But she just couldn't bring herself to spend the rest of her life with someone she didn't love. She longed for someone who could make her heart race with just a smile—someone like Silas. As soon as the thought of him crossed her mind, she pushed it away.

Being in the third trimester of her pregnancy, Cecelia was greatly showing. A protective hand pressed to her abdomen as she lowered herself to the chair facing Gisella's desk. "Ah… Much better." Once she was settled, her gaze met Gisella's. "I think I'm carrying a little footballer. All he does is kick."

Gisella smiled. Leave it to her youngest sister to distract her. "He has to get in his exercise. When he's born, he'll be ready to join a football team."

"I know you're joking but you're probably right. I can attest that he loves to kick. He does it off and on all day. And then at night when you would think he'd quiet down, he only gets more active."

"Sounds like you're enjoying your pregnancy."

She smiled and nodded. "It's been amazing. I haven't had to read a pregnancy book because I swear Antoine has read them all. He likes to inform me about my pregnancy."

"Sounds like he's an involved father."

"He definitely is. Today he told me the baby is the size of an eggplant, or was it a butternut squash? Can you imagine?" Cecelia smiled and shook her head.

Gisella let out a laugh. "It's great to hear that you two are so happy."

"Enough about me and my vegetable di-lemma. What's been happening with you? I saw the gala and the awards ceremony. Congratula-tions. It was a huge success."

She nodded. "Everything went really well, but I couldn't have pulled it off if it wasn't for Silas. He was amazing."

Cecelia's eyes widened. "So that's why you called off the engagement."

"What?" She wondered what her sister was implying. "We called it off because neither of us wanted to marry the other."

"Because you're in love with Silas."

"I am not." The denial was a little too quick.

"I saw the photos online of you and him to-gether going to the theater. You looked radiant. In fact, I've never seen you happier. I can't help but wonder if that's the reason you called off the engagement."

She shook her head. "I just realized that I couldn't live with a loveless marriage and Matis felt the same way."

"But if the groom were to be Silas, would you feel differently?"

Yes! Definitely yes.

She'd never believed in love at first sight. Silas had changed all of that. Or in their case maybe it was second sight—once she'd figured out that he wasn't irresponsible but rather a real-life hero.

She gave herself a mental shake. Thinking of him wouldn't help matters. It would only make her heart ache more. "It doesn't matter. It can never happen. Remember there's a clause in the charter that says the heir to the throne can only marry another royal."

Cecelia stared intently at her as though she was trying to read her thoughts. "It sounds like you've given this a lot of thought."

Gisella shrugged. "Like I said, it doesn't matter."

"I think it matters a great deal. You're in love with him and you're finding every reason to fight it. My question is why. If you love him, why aren't you fighting to have him in your life?"

Exasperation knotted up her stomach. "It

doesn't matter. Silas is moving on with his life. I just heard that the merger he's had in the works is moving forward. It's what he wants most."

"How do you know?"

"Because he told me how important his business is to him."

Cecelia was quiet for a moment as though digesting this information. "Okay. Even if it's not Silas you marry, you still need to fight for your right to choose who you marry. No one should have to spend the rest of their life with someone they don't love."

Gisella agreed wholeheartedly. "Don't you think I know that, but how am I to fight the kingdom's charter? It's the reason our own brother stepped out of line for the crown."

Cecelia gave her a thoughtful look. "Perhaps you have to be the smarter sibling. I've never known you to give up on anything you truly want. Why are you so willing to give up now?"

It was true. She could be tenacious. But was there a way to fix this? Could she have the charter amended?

"I don't know." Gisella's mind raced as she searched for an answer.

"You're going to become queen in the new year. You can do anything you set your mind to do. Listen to the little voice in your head. You'll find a way." Cecelia got to her feet. "I need to go see if Antoine got settled in our room. And I think you have some work to do."

When Cecelia left the room, Gisella couldn't believe she was taking advice from the sister who had always been known as the wild child in the family. And yet she couldn't dismiss what Cecelia had said.

Gisella reached for her phone and pulled up a picture of her with Silas atop the Empire State Building. They'd been so happy then. And she missed him so much. She could no longer deny that she loved him with all of her heart.

And then she knew what must be done. She got to her feet and rushed to the library. She'd been tutored a lot over the past year about the kingdom's policies and most especially about the charter. There was something in there about how to change it. It wouldn't be easy but it was possible. She just had to verify a thing or two.

A couple of hours later, Gisella was armed with the knowledge she needed. Her footsteps were muffled by a long red runner that ran throughout the downstairs. The hallways were quite wide, allowing for easy passage for the royal family and the couple of hundred staff members that worked within the palace walls.

After being gone for so long, she saw the palace with fresh eyes. She took in the closed doors that lined each side of the hallway as well as the cream-colored couches that were situated periodically along the wall. In addition, there were ornate pieces of furniture as well as priceless statues and large ceramic vases that were gifts from various nations. The whole palace was steeped in tradition.

At last, she reached her destination. Gisella opened the solid wood door and stepped into the outer office, where the king's secretary worked long hours. It was a well-known part of the honored position. The bald gentleman with gold wire-frame glasses continued his work, making her wait.

A couple of minutes later, he glanced up. His eyes momentarily widened. He scrambled to his feet and bowed to her. When he straightened, he said, "Your Royal Highness, how may I help you?"

"I need to speak with the King."

"Let me announce your presence. Wait here." He disappeared inside the King's inner sanctum only to return a minute later. "The King will see you now."

"Thank you."

The secretary escorted her into the King's office. "Your Majesty… Princess Gisella."

When she was admitted to his office, she found that the Queen was there as well. She hadn't anticipated dealing with both of them at the same time, but it would save her the time of having to repeat herself.

The secretary backed out, never turning his back to the royals. And then the door softly snicked shut. The three of them were alone.

His father was seated behind his large oak desk with her mother standing next to him. In front of him sat a large stack of papers. The King didn't like modern technology and preferred paper memos and reports.

"Sit." The King looked at her expectantly.

After bowing to her parents, she straightened and leveled her shoulders. "I prefer to stand."

"What is this about?" her mother asked.

Gisella's insides shivered with nerves. She'd never been so bold before, but if she was to be an effective queen, she needed to learn to be direct and forceful when the need arose.

"I need to speak with you both about the kingdom's charter."

Her father's dark brows drew together. "What about it?"

Her mother stood next to her father with an equally puzzled look on her face. She remained quiet as she awaited Gisella's next words.

"It's time for a change."

Without even hearing about the change she wanted to make, her father shook his head. "It isn't going to happen."

"Gisella," the Queen said, "how could you propose such a thing? The charter is never changed. It is the backbone of our kingdom."

"Surely you have to understand that times are different now than they were when the charter was written three centuries ago. The world has changed."

"What has gotten into you?" the King asked. "I've never heard you talk like this before."

The Queen pressed her hands to her hips. "I told you that lengthy trip to the States wasn't a good idea."

"Please stop." Gisella grew frustrated with her parents for shooting down her idea without even hearing her out. "You don't even know what I want to change."

"I beg to differ with you," the Queen said. "You want to remove the stipulation that you must marry a royal."

Gisella struggled to keep from gaping at her mother. She knew her mother was astute, but she hadn't realized just how sharp she was. She lifted her chin upward ever so slightly. "Yes, I do."

The King shook his head. "If that were possible it would have been done for your brother."

"I don't think my brother asked for the charter to be amended."

"Yes, he did," the King responded. "And I told

him the same thing I'm telling you. It can't be done."

And this is where all her time being tutored about the driest subject of the rule of law and order of the kingdom came in handy. She began to explain to them how the charter worked and what was needed to amend it.

The King and Queen were astonished that she had amassed such knowledge. They were impressed that she'd absorbed most everything her eighty-year-old scholar had drilled into her day after day. But she knew to be an effective ruler, she needed all of the tools made available to her.

"So, you see," Gisella said, "it will take the unanimous agreement of the King and the royal privy council."

"You're asking too much," the Queen said. "Traditions are to be adhered to."

"I cannot… No. I will not agree to an arranged marriage. I will not subject myself to a life without love. So, either modify the charter or I will have no recourse but to reject the crown."

There was a collective gasp from her parents. She didn't care. This was just too much. She meant every word that she'd spoken.

Before her parents could mount a defense, Gisella turned on her heels and strode away. She didn't know if her plan would work. Getting a unanimous vote would be difficult, but not impossible. It was the only chance she had of finding true happiness.

Her thoughts turned to Silas. If only things were different—if only they weren't two totally driven people who lived so far apart. She couldn't ask him to give up his company any more than he could ask her to give up the crown.

But would she walk away from the crown if the charter wasn't amended? She honestly didn't know the answer. Until she'd met Silas she didn't know how important it was to love your life partner—she didn't know what a difference love could make. And now that she knew, she couldn't accept less.

CHAPTER SEVENTEEN

Christmas Eve had arrived.

The flight from New York to Rydiania had been long but uneventful. Silas had spent the whole flight thinking about Gisella. He'd never had such an intense experience with anyone.

He knew Gisella felt the same way toward him. It was in her smile. And in the way she'd agreed to sneak off with him in order to explore their growing feelings for each other.

But would all of that be enough for her to turn her back on her family, her country and her destiny? He understood how important the crown was to her, but he also understood that this thing that happened between them was unique. And he didn't think it would ever happen to him again. Not with anyone else.

If he didn't go through with this plan, he would regret it for the rest of his life. And yet he didn't like being in a place of not knowing the outcome of something. When it came to business, he was an expert at achieving his goal, but this venture was far from business.

His hand moved to his pocket where he had Gisella's Christmas presents. He could only hope they would open a door to her heart so he could step through.

On this starry night, his plane touched down. There was a car service waiting for him. He followed the chauffer to the dark sedan.

"Where are we headed?" the driver asked with a heavy accent.

To see the woman of my dreams.

"The Rydiania Palace."

"The palace?" There was a note of surprise in his voice. "Do you have an invitation?"

"I do not."

The driver shook his head. "Sir, they don't allow tourists on the palace grounds, especially at this hour."

"Don't worry. You just get me there and I'll take care of the rest."

The driver sent him a look like he was certain Silas didn't know what he was talking about, but to his credit, he didn't put up an argument. With the luggage in the trunk, they set off for the Rydiania Palace.

Even though the sun had long ago set, it was still bright out. Between the starry sky with a full moon and the ground covered with a fresh layer of snow, there was a lot of light. He continued to stare out the window as they passed by the exit to a city.

A little way down the highway, they exited. After stopping at an intersection, the car merged onto a single roadway that wound its way into a small village. It was filled with unique shops and cozy restaurants. He imagined in the daylight hours that the village would be busy with tourists.

On the outskirts of the village sat a park. At that late hour there was no one there. Not quite a mile down the road, the car slowed to a stop. In front of the car stood a very tall wrought iron gate. Guards in deep purple uniforms with black hats stood in front of the gate. To either side of the gate were guard shacks that were much more than shacks, because no shack looked that nice.

"I hope you know what you're doing," the driver said.

"Me too," Silas muttered under his breath. He rolled down his window to speak to the armed guard in a royal uniform. "I'm here to see Princess Gisella."

"Is she expecting you?"

"No. But if you will tell her that Silas is here, I'm sure she'll agree to see me."

"Sir, the royal family does not see unexpected

guests. You'll have to call and make an appointment."

This couldn't be the way things ended. He hadn't come all of this way just to be turned away at the gate. "Just call her."

"No, sir. Please leave."

When the driver put the car in Reverse, Silas said, "Don't leave. Wait. I'll fix this."

And then he did something he had been longing to do since Gisella left New York. He pulled his phone from his pocket. And he dialed Gisella's number. He hoped she'd pick up.

The phone rang once. And then twice. And then a third time. No answer. By the fifth ring, it switched to voice mail. He disconnected the call.

This couldn't be happening. Had he really come all this way to be turned away at the gate? His mind raced with some way to fix this.

Buzz.

He glanced down at his phone. It was Gisella. His heart picked up its pace as he pressed the phone to his ear. "Hello."

"Silas?"

"Yes, it's me."

"I'm so surprised to hear from you. It's good to hear your voice. You sound like you're so close."

"That might be because I'm at the gate."

"What?" Her voice rose. "You're here? In Rydiania?"

A smile pulled at his lips. "I am."

"Really?" Her excited voice told him everything he needed to know.

"If you would tell the guard to let me in, you could see for yourself."

"Of course."

"Gisella?" Silence. "Gisella, are you there?"

The line went dead.

The phone inside the guard shack rang. The guard frowned at him as he went to answer the phone. The conversation was short.

Two guards moved toward the gate with precise movements that must have been practiced for many, many hours. They moved in unison and swung the giant gates open.

"You really do have connections." The driver sounded quite impressed.

The car rolled slowly along the smoothly paved roadway. Silas stared out the window at the field of snow as the full moon hung low in the sky. The moonlight sparkled off the fresh snow as though it were a field of tiny twinkling diamonds.

His heart raced as he thought of seeing Gisella again. At the same time, his gut knotted up as he wondered if she felt the same way about him. And if she did, how were they going to make this relationship work?

Would she consider stepping away from her

life of royalty to have a life filled with love? He honestly didn't know the answer. But he knew he couldn't return home without giving their relationship a true and honest chance.

Outside the car window the gigantic palace came into view. There were floodlights that lit up the whole place as though it were daylight outside. He knew it was for security reasons. Still, he wouldn't appreciate the constant bright light when he was trying to sleep. But he supposed they would have blackout curtains.

The palace was built with one light gray stone upon another. At the corners were impressive round turrets that soared up past the palace walls, giving a spectacular view of the area for miles. He imagined centuries ago the towers would have held guards on constant guard for any attack. Now they just looked impressive.

In the front center of the palace was a large purple-and-white flag that fluttered in the breeze. The car turned sharply and pulled to a stop beneath a portico. His door was opened by a butler or footman or whatever their title might be. The gentleman was dressed in a black-and-white formal suit and he wore a serious expression.

Silas drew in a deep breath. This was it. This was what he knew would be his one and only chance to convince Gisella that they had something special—too special to let it go.

He made his way up the few steps to the red runner that led him inside the grand palace. His heart pounded as he struggled to come up with the right words to convince Gisella that they were worth any sacrifice.

"Please wait here." The footman turned and walked away.

For the moment, he was all alone in the foyer. It gave him a chance to take it all in. He didn't think it was possible but the inside was even more impressive than the outside.

The white marble floor gleamed. The overhead lights reflected off it. He lifted his chin in order to take in the giant glass dome in the ceiling that let in the moonlight. In the center of the room a giant crystal chandelier was suspended. Its many lights made the crystals shimmer. It was quite captivating.

To either side of the grand foyer were twin staircases that were lined with deep purple carpet that led to the second floor.

But what took center stage was the giant Christmas tree that was situated between the two staircases. It made the Christmas tree he'd had in his penthouse look dismal by comparison. Gisella hadn't exaggerated when she'd said it was a big tree. It soared up to the second floor.

It was wrapped in purple twinkling lights. The branches were trimmed with hundreds of white and silver glass ornaments. And at the tiptop was a white angel.

As beautiful as the tree was, he noticed that it lacked any personality. His mother's tree had ornaments they'd collected over the years. Each one had a specific memory. Some of the ornaments he'd made as a kid as a gift for his mother. Now when he saw them, he was a bit embarrassed by his lack of artistic skill. He'd mentioned tossing them out, but his mother had vehemently refused. She said the imperfections were what made them perfect.

The sound of footsteps echoed across the marble floor. He turned his head to the side to see the footman return. Behind him were an older couple, but no sign of Gisella.

The beating of his heart stilled. Did she have a change of heart? But then he recalled the excitement in her voice when she learned he was there to see her. Something else was going on.

"May I present the King and Queen." The footman bowed before making his departure.

Gisella's parents gave him an assessing look. He bowed his head. He wasn't sure if it was protocol for him to speak first or them. He decided to let them make the first move.

As the awkward silence stretched on, his buttoned shirt collar grew tighter. He resisted the urge to loosen his tie and unbutton his shirt collar. He refused to let her parents know their presence unnerved him.

"I guess we should thank you for helping out with the gala," the King said.

"I enjoyed working with your daughter."

"You mean Princess Gisella." The Queen arched a brow.

"Ah, yes, Princess Gisella." He'd momentarily forgotten that her parents were strict about protocol. Or were they sending him a signal that they would never approve of his daughter being involved with him? "She had a lot of great ideas."

"And what brings you here on Christmas Eve?" The King crossed his arms.

Silas hadn't expected to be interrogated by her parents so he didn't have an answer readily available. And so he latched onto the first thought that came to mind.

"I didn't get a chance to give Gi…erm, Princess Gisella her Christmas present."

Another awkward silence ensued. Silas couldn't help but wonder if conversations with the King and Queen were always so stilted. But if this was what he had to go through in order to reach Gisella, he'd do it.

"You care about our daughter," the King said.

Silas wasn't sure if that was a statement or a

question. Either way, he was going to confirm the King's suspicion. "Yes, sir. I do."

"You do realize that very soon she's going to be the queen of this kingdom." A note of warning was in the King's voice.

"I understand, but it doesn't change how I feel about her."

"What are your intentions where Gisella is concerned?" The King's intent stare bore into him.

He leveled his shoulders as he met the King's gaze. His heart beat faster. His palms grew clammy. And the collar on his shirt grew tighter. "I don't know, sir. That's up to Gi…erm, the Princess."

"Did someone call my name?"

Everyone turned to the staircase, where Gisella stood in a pale pink dress that stopped a couple of inches before her knees. The bodice was studded with little crystals that twinkled in the light.

He swallowed hard. No woman had ever looked so beautiful. His heart pounded against his ribs.

Her long brown loose curls fell down over her shoulders. There was a smile on her face that was so brilliant it lit up the whole room. In white heels studded with rhinestones, she continued down the steps. Time slowed down as she took one step at a time.

All the while his present for her burned a hole in his pocket, but he couldn't rush things. He had to take his time. He had to do this right. There wouldn't be any second chances.

CHAPTER EIGHTEEN

HE'D NEVER LOOKED sexier in his blue suit and tie.

Her heart pitter-pattered.

Gisella couldn't take her gaze off him. Her knees felt like they were made of gelatin as she made her way to him. She held herself back from throwing her arms around him. She had absolutely no idea why he was there on Christmas Eve of all times.

Even if he cared about her like she suspected, she was still the Crown Princess. And as much as she tried to imagine turning her back on the crown and walking away, she could never do it—even if it meant never marrying.

Being a leader was as much a part of her as Silas's business was a part of him. Could he accept giving up his life in New York and moving to Rydiania? She didn't think so.

She halted her thoughts. She was getting too far ahead. First, she needed to see why he was here. Maybe he was just there for a visit. Nothing more.

She came to a stop in front of him. "Hello, Silas."

"Your Highness." He bowed his head.

"Silas, stop. You don't have to do that when it's just you and me." When he turned his head and looked around, she said, "If you're looking for my parents, they left."

His face relaxed as a smile lifted the corners of his lips. "You look beautiful."

"Thank you. You're looking quite handsome too." She clenched her hands together to keep from reaching out to him.

"The gala was a huge success."

"It was. We've gained a lot of new sponsors for next year. Research is going to double in an effort to save the bees and our planet. And how was it for you? Did you impress your business associate?"

Silas nodded. "He liked what he saw and he was most impressed with you."

"So the merger is moving ahead?" The breath stilled in her lungs as she awaited his answer.

She knew how important his business was to him. She didn't think there was any reason he would give it up—not even for her. But what she wanted most was for him to be happy—even if it was without her.

"It is. I should thank you for the help."

She shook her head. "I didn't have anything to do with it. It was all you."

"But you impressed Mr. Carr. After he met you, he was very agreeable to the terms of the merger." His gaze met hers. "But I didn't come here to talk about the merger."

"Why are you here?" Her heart pounded.

"To apologize for pushing you away at the gala. I shouldn't have acted that way."

His apology surprised and pleased her. "Apology accepted."

She wondered if that was the only reason he was there. She hoped not. But as silence dragged on, she worried that the spark—the magic—they'd experienced in New York had fizzled out.

"I've missed you." His voice was soft.

"I've missed you too. I called your office the other day, but you weren't there."

"Why didn't you call my cell phone?"

She shrugged. "I wasn't sure you wanted to talk to me."

"Then why did you call the office?"

"Oh, just checking up on some damage at the gala. Nothing major." She realized that wasn't the whole truth. If she wasn't willing to be brutally honest with him, how did she expect him to be honest with her? "The truth is that it was just an excuse. I really wanted to talk to you."

"Again. Why didn't you call my cell phone?" He wasn't going to make this easy for her.

She swallowed hard. "After the way we left things at the gala, I… I didn't know what to say."

He took a step closer. "Gisella, I'm so sorry. I never meant to make you feel that way. It was just with seeing you with that guy, I guess I was a bit jealous."

"You were?" A smile tugged at the corners of her lips.

"And why do you look so pleased?"

She stepped toward him. She lifted up on her tiptoes. "Because it means I can do this."

She leaned her head toward him. He met her somewhere in the middle and pressed his lips to hers. Oh, how she'd missed this—missed him. So very much!

His arms reached out to her. His hands gripped her hips, drawing her closer. She followed his lead and leaned into him. Her curves pressed into his hard plains.

They fit together perfectly—as though they'd been made for each other. His lips moved over hers and she opened up to him. She knew in that moment that she never wanted to live without him again.

He was her best friend, her lover and the other half of her heart. Her hands moved up over his broad shoulders and wrapped around the back of his neck. Her fingers forked their way through his hair. All the while her heart pounded so hard that it echoed in her ears. If this was a dream, she didn't want to wake up.

And then Silas pulled back. Her eyes fluttered open. She stared up at him in confusion. "What's wrong?"

He backed up. He averted his gaze. "I shouldn't be kissing you."

"Why not?" She thought it was a mighty fine way to spend their time.

"You know why."

"If you're worried about my family—"

"I'm not." He sighed. "I can't believe I have to point this out, but you're supposed to marry that guy, remember?"

"His name is Matis." She stepped closer. "And you don't have to worry about him."

"Well, Matis surely wouldn't approve of this." With an uncomfortable look on his face, Silas held out his hand, stopping her from wrapping her arms around him.

Gisella couldn't help but smile. "I don't think Matis would feel one way or the other about us kissing."

Silas's brows rose. "I know you said that it's supposed to be some sort of arranged marriage, but isn't that taking things a bit too casual?"

Her smile broadened. "He won't care what you and I do because Matis and I agreed to go our separate ways."

"Really?"

She nodded. "After my time in New York, I realized I couldn't commit to a marriage without love."

There was a pause as though he was trying to come to terms with what she was telling him. "You figured that out while you and I were together?"

"I did." And as much fun as she was having bantering with him, she knew a more in-depth answer was required. "I figured out a whole lot while we were together."

The hint of a smile shone on his face. "And what would that be?"

"That life is so much easier when you have someone who makes you smile by your side."

His smile broadened. "You think so?"

"I do. And I figured out that life is too long to spend it with someone I don't love."

"Anything else?"

"That if I marry, I want the person to be my best friend and someone I'm madly in love with."

He blew out a deep breath. "You're certainly asking for a lot."

"Perhaps. Do you think I'll be able to find someone like that?"

"Does that mean you're looking?"

"Are you applying for the position?"

He reached out and drew her close. "I've never felt so close to anyone." He stared into her eyes. "I love you."

"I love you too."

He lowered his head and kissed her again. She hoped this was just the start of a lifetime of his kisses. She would never get enough of him. Not ever.

Much too soon he pulled back.

She sighed. "This is becoming a habit with you."

"What?"

"Pulling away much too soon."

"I want this to work." He waved his hand between the two of them. "But how can we make that happen? After all, I don't have a drop of royal blood in me."

"Oh, I see." She struggled not to smile. "Well, I've been very busy since I got home and there has been a change to Rydiania's charter."

"What does that mean?"

"That by royal decree, I don't have to marry someone of royal lineage." She stepped up to him and rested her hands on his chest. "How would you feel about becoming a duke?" The words were out of her mouth before she realized the implication of her words. "I'm sorry. I shouldn't have said that."

"Why?"

"Because I can't ask you to walk away from your business. I know how important it is to you. It's the same way I feel about my work here."

"I had a lot of time to think after you left."

She stared deeply into his eyes. "And what did you decide?"

"Maybe I'll show you." He withdrew two small packages from his pockets. "Pick one."

She pointed to his right hand. He handed it to her and she opened it. Inside the small box she found a tiny replica of the Empire State Building.

She gasped. "How did you know that I've been thinking of our time there?"

"I didn't but I was hoping it was as special to you as it was for me."

"I love it!" She lifted her gaze to his. "Thank you for being so thoughtful."

"I wanted you to have something to remind you of your time in New York."

"It will. I'll always keep it close by."

"And now for your other gift." He held the small box out to her.

There was a slight tremble in her hands. Her mind raced with what might be inside. She took it from him and ripped the paper from it.

Her mouth gaped when she found a black velvet box.

Is this a ring box? No... No. It must be something else. Perhaps a necklace. Yes, that must be it. Because there's no way there is a diamond ring inside. Right?

She lifted her gaze to his. She didn't know what she expected to see in his eyes, but what she found was love. It warmed her chest and set her heart aflutter.

He took the velvet box from her. He led her over to the Christmas tree, where he dropped down on one knee. She let out a gasp. She pressed a shaky hand to her mouth as she blinked back happy tears.

This was really happening. He was proposing. More tears rushed to her eyes, blurring her vision.

He lifted his chin until their gazes met. "Gisella, you've changed my life ever since our first video chat. I never thought when I met you in person that it would be such a profound moment. Although I have to admit that you weren't too thrilled with me at our first meeting."

"How was I to know that you were off being a hero?" She smiled at him.

"Thank you for giving me another chance. You showed me that no one is perfect, but you don't have to be for someone to care about you.

You've shown me that love doesn't have to be earned. It can simply exist."

Her heart was beating rapidly as she struggled to keep her emotions under wraps. Who knew that Silas could be so good with words. With every sentence he uttered, she felt herself falling even more in love with him.

"You are the light in my life. Without you, my life is gray and dark. I can't imagine living my life without you. Will you marry me?"

The word *yes* teetered on the tip of her tongue, but she knew it wasn't that easy. This marriage would change everything. She had to make sure Silas knew what he was getting himself into. "How will we make this work?"

The smile slipped from his face as he stood. "Are you saying no?"

She shook her head. "I'm asking how we would make a marriage work. I can't leave Rydiania. Being their queen is my destiny. And the company you built is in New York and soon in Los Angeles. How will we ever see each other?"

He straightened. "I gave that some thought on my plane ride. I'm thinking that Rydiania could use its own top-notch PR firm. What do you think?"

Was he serious? By the look on his face, he was. "I think that would be wonderful. And I'm certain the palace will help keep it busy. But does this mean you're selling your company in the States?"

He shook his head. "I'm thinking of continuing to expand the business. Obviously, I'll have to put people in charge of each office, but I don't see why I can't move the headquarters to Rydiania."

She was impressed with how much thought he'd put into this proposal. Happy tears splashed onto her cheeks. "In that case, ask me again."

He knelt down on one knee again and held the ring out to her. "Princess Gisella, you are the queen of my heart. Will you marry me?"

"Yes." Her voice trembled with emotions as more tears rolled down her cheeks. "Yes, I'll marry you. I love you."

He slipped the ring onto her finger and straightened. "I love you too."

He lowered his head and claimed her lips with his own. Who said that fairy tales didn't come true? She'd found her Prince Charming and she was never going to let him go.

EPILOGUE

Two years later, Rydiania Palace

CHRISTMAS WISHES REALLY did come true.

Outside the palace it was snowing. Everything was coated in a white fluffy snow. Queen Gisella stared out at the tranquil morning. Luckily all of the family was already at the palace so she didn't have to worry about anyone being out on the icy roads.

In her arms was a hungry, crying baby. "Just a little longer and you'll have a bottle."

The infant found her tiny fist to suck on. Gisella knew the respite wouldn't last long. She hoped Silas would hurry.

She turned and moved to an armchair next to the Christmas tree. All of the presents had been opened except for one very special gift. It was still under the tree, where it would remain for just a little longer.

Gisella sat down carefully so as not to jostle her firstborn. Her Royal Highness Princess Penelope was exactly five days old. And she had her father's dark hair and, so far, she had her mother's blue eyes. She was told it would take a few months to see if they would remain blue or not.

Almost two-year-old Prince Markos toddled over to her. Her adorable nephew had gone from being held to walking. He had no time for crawling. He kept her sister Cecilia and brother-in-law Antoine on their toes. Gisella had never seen her sister look so happy. Parenthood agreed with them, which would explain why Cecelia was already three months into her next pregnancy.

As Markos toddled off toward his father, her attention turned to her brother Istvan and his wife, Indigo. They were the only couple without children. Gisella had assumed they chose not to have any kids, but then last night at dinner, they'd announced that they were now trying for a baby. It made Gisella's parents beam. Grandparenthood totally agreed with them. Now that they were able to slow down, they doted on their grandchildren. Who'd have ever thought her mother would be so good with babies?

Her other sister, Beatrix, held her stepdaughter, Evi, as they played with a pink teddy bear. Beatrix and Rez, the Duke of Kaspar, had recently gotten married at a small and intimate ceremony at Rez's country estate. Their mother had been disappointed that it wasn't a bigger affair at the palace, but thankfully she hadn't made a big fuss.

It was also announced last night that Beatrix was going to adopt Evi. Her sister beamed with love for the little girl. Gisella couldn't remember ever seeing her sister so happy. In fact, all of her siblings were happy and in love. In the end, love had won out over duty. Gisella didn't see why love and duty couldn't coexist happily within the palace walls.

When Penelope started to fuss again, Gisella placed the baby on her shoulder and gently patted her tiny bottom in hopes that it would distract her daughter until her father returned with her bottle.

"Are you having a good Christmas?" Gisella's mother-in-law sat down next to her.

A smile immediately pulled at the corners of Gisella's lips. "It's the best. And I'm so happy you're here to share it with us."

Silas's mother had finally agreed to move in with them. It wasn't like there wasn't enough room at the palace. The whole family was staying in the palace and there were still plenty of rooms to spare.

"I just can't believe I live in a palace. My friends back in New York are so impressed."

"You know that you're welcome to invite them here anytime you want."

"Thank you."

"You don't have to thank me. This is now your home too. I know Silas rests so much easier with you close by."

"Speaking of my son, do you know where he went?"

"He went to get Penelope a bottle."

His mother lowered her voice. "Don't you have people to do that for you?"

"Not today. Today we are on our own while the staff spends time with their families."

The only staff was a minimal security staff. Luckily the kitchen staff had prepped everything for dinner and left instructions on how to heat it all up. Hopefully it wouldn't be too hard. Though she had heard that Cecelia was learning to cook so maybe she'd keep them from ruining the meal.

Penelope was done waiting for her food. She let out a loud wail. As though responding to his daughter's demand, Silas rushed into the room with a warmed bottle.

Once Penelope was greedily sucking on the bottle, Gisella leaned back in the chair and stared down at her daughter with her rosy lips and chubby cheeks. There was a contented look on her face.

As the Queen, it was expected that nannies would do the bulk of raising her daughter. It was the way she'd been raised, but Gisella was bucking that tradition. She had worked out a plan to have her family help with royal responsibilities. They all understood if they pulled together that they would all have more time for their growing families.

Even Cecelia and her husband, Antoine, had made the decision to move from the South of France to Rydiania to be closer to the family. Going forward, they would be a part of the working royals. They wanted their child to grow up with their cousins. Gisella loved that their family was growing and flourishing. The cousins would have so much fun together. Oh, the trouble they'd get themselves into. Gisella was looking forward to all of it.

Silas drew a chair up next to her. "She's so beautiful, just like her mother."

"I think she has a lot of her father in her." Gisella noticed the pleased look on his face. "By the way, there's one more package under the tree. Would you mind grabbing it?"

He moved to the tree and picked up a smallish box in red foil paper and a silver bow. When he sat back down, he asked, "Who's it for? I don't see a name on it."

"It's for you."

"Me? But I have everything I want. I have my two favorite ladies next to me."

She loved his flattery. It never got old because she knew it came from a place of love. "Just open it."

His brows lifted. "Pushy, aren't we?"

She rolled her eyes but didn't say anything as he shook the package as though trying to guess what was inside.

"It must be a new tie. Am I right?"

"I'm not telling you so you might as well open it."

So he finally ripped the paper off the slim box and then lifted the lid. Inside were some folded papers. He sent her a questioning glance. She gestured for him to pick them up.

He tentatively did as she asked as though he was worried about their contents. And then he started reading. It was a complete history of his family or as complete as they could make it. The project had started with a DNA analysis and from there she'd appointed someone to trace back through the decades and centuries for his ancestors. It wasn't an easy task because some of the records had been lost. But her team hadn't given up and eventually they were able to trace his lineage back many generations.

When she heard him take a quick gasp of air, she knew he'd reached the pivotal part of the research. He turned to her. "Does this mean I have royal blood?"

She smiled and nodded. "On your father's side many generations ago his many-greats-grandfather was a king, making you a prince."

"I had no idea."

"But I did."

"How?" His gaze searched hers.

"Because since the day you took me to decorate your Christmas tree you've been the prince of my heart."

He leaned over and kissed her. "And you're the queen of my heart. Merry Christmas."

"Merry Christmas."

* * * * *

*If you missed the previous story in
the Princesses of Rydiania trilogy,
then check out*
Royal Mom for the Duke's Daughter

*And if you enjoyed this story,
check out these other great reads
from Jennifer Faye*

His Accidentally Pregnant Princess
Second Chance with the Bridesmaid
It Started with a Royal Kiss

All available now!